MORE PRAISE FOR BABYMOUSE!

"Sassy, smart . . .
Babymouse is here
to stay."
—The Horn Book Magazine

"Young readers
will happily
fall in line."
—Kirkus Reviews

"The brother-sister creative team hits the mark
with humor, sweetness, and characters so genuine
they can pass for real kids." —Booklist

"Babymouse is spunky, ambitious,
and, at times, a total dweeb."
—School Library Journal

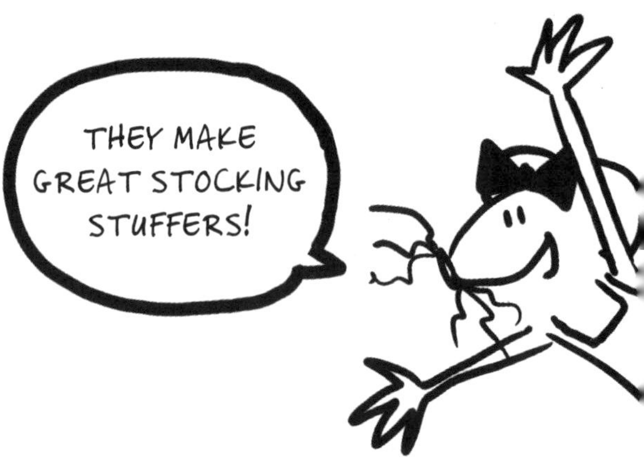
THEY MAKE GREAT STOCKING STUFFERS!

BE SURE TO READ **ALL** THE **BABYMOUSE** BOOKS:

#1 BABYMOUSE: Queen of the World!
#2 BABYMOUSE: Our Hero
#3 BABYMOUSE: Beach Babe
#4 BABYMOUSE: Rock Star
#5 BABYMOUSE: Heartbreaker
#6 CAMP BABYMOUSE
#7 BABYMOUSE: Skater Girl
#8 BABYMOUSE: Puppy Love
#9 BABYMOUSE: Monster Mash
#10 BABYMOUSE: The Musical
#11 BABYMOUSE: Dragonslayer
#12 BABYMOUSE: Burns Rubber
#13 BABYMOUSE: Cupcake Tycoon
#14 BABYMOUSE: Mad Scientist
#15 A Very BABYMOUSE Christmas

A VERY BABYMOUSE CHRISTMAS

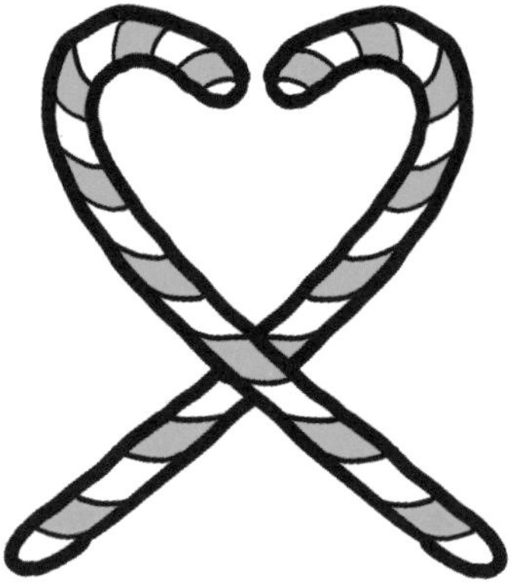

BY JENNIFER L. HOLM & MATTHEW HOLM

RANDOM HOUSE NEW YORK

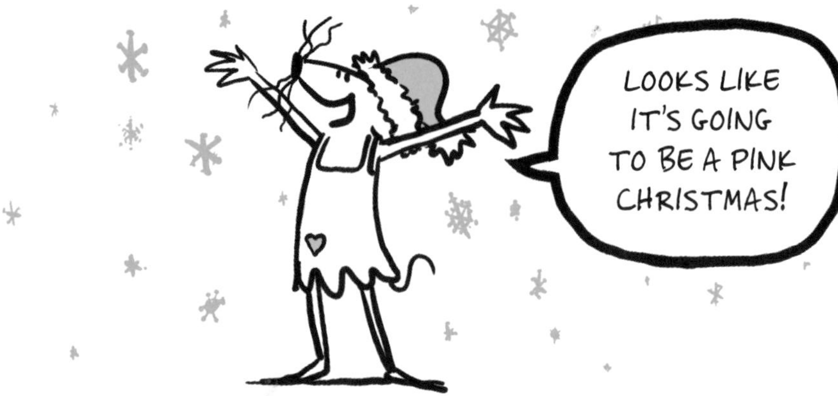
LOOKS LIKE IT'S GOING TO BE A PINK CHRISTMAS!

Published in the United States by Random House Children's Books, a division of Random House, Inc., New York.

Random House and the colophon are registered trademarks of Random House, Inc.

Visit us on the Web! www.randomhouse.com/kids

Educators and librarians, for a variety of teaching tools, visit us at www.randomhouse.com/teachers

Babymouse.com

Library of Congress Cataloging-in-Publication Data
Holm, Jennifer L.
Babymouse : a very Babymouse Christmas / by Jennifer L. Holm and Matthew Holm. — 1st ed.
p. cm.
Summary: A spunky mouse with an active imagination is determined to get the latest electronic gadget for Christmas even if she has to outfox Santa himself to get it.
ISBN 978-0-375-86779-8 (trade) — ISBN 978-0-375-96779-5 (lib. bdg.)
1. Graphic novels. [1. Graphic novels. 2. Christmas—Fiction. 3. Gifts—Fiction. 4. Imagination—Fiction. 5. Mice—Fiction. 6. Animals—Fiction. 7. Humorous stories.] I. Holm, Matthew. II. Title. III. Title: Very Babymouse Christmas.
PZ7.7.H65 Bac 2011 741.5'973—dc22 2010027988

MANUFACTURED IN MALAYSIA

10 9 8 7 6 5 4 3 2 1

First Edition

Random House Children's Books supports the First Amendment and celebrates the right to read.

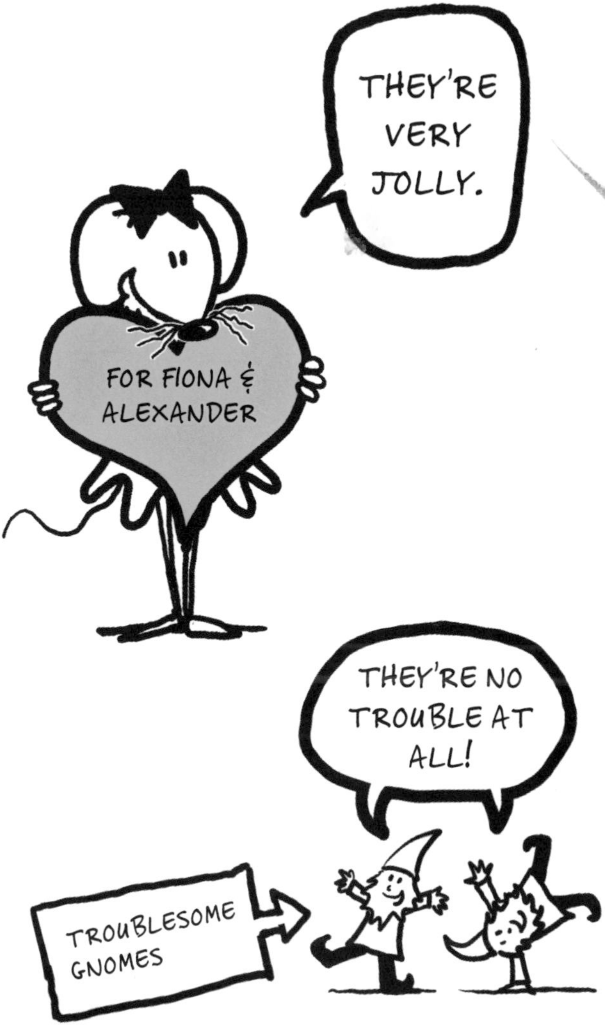
THEY'RE VERY JOLLY.
FOR FIONA & ALEXANDER
THEY'RE NO TROUBLE AT ALL!
TROUBLESOME GNOMES

A Visit from St. Nick

By the Narrator

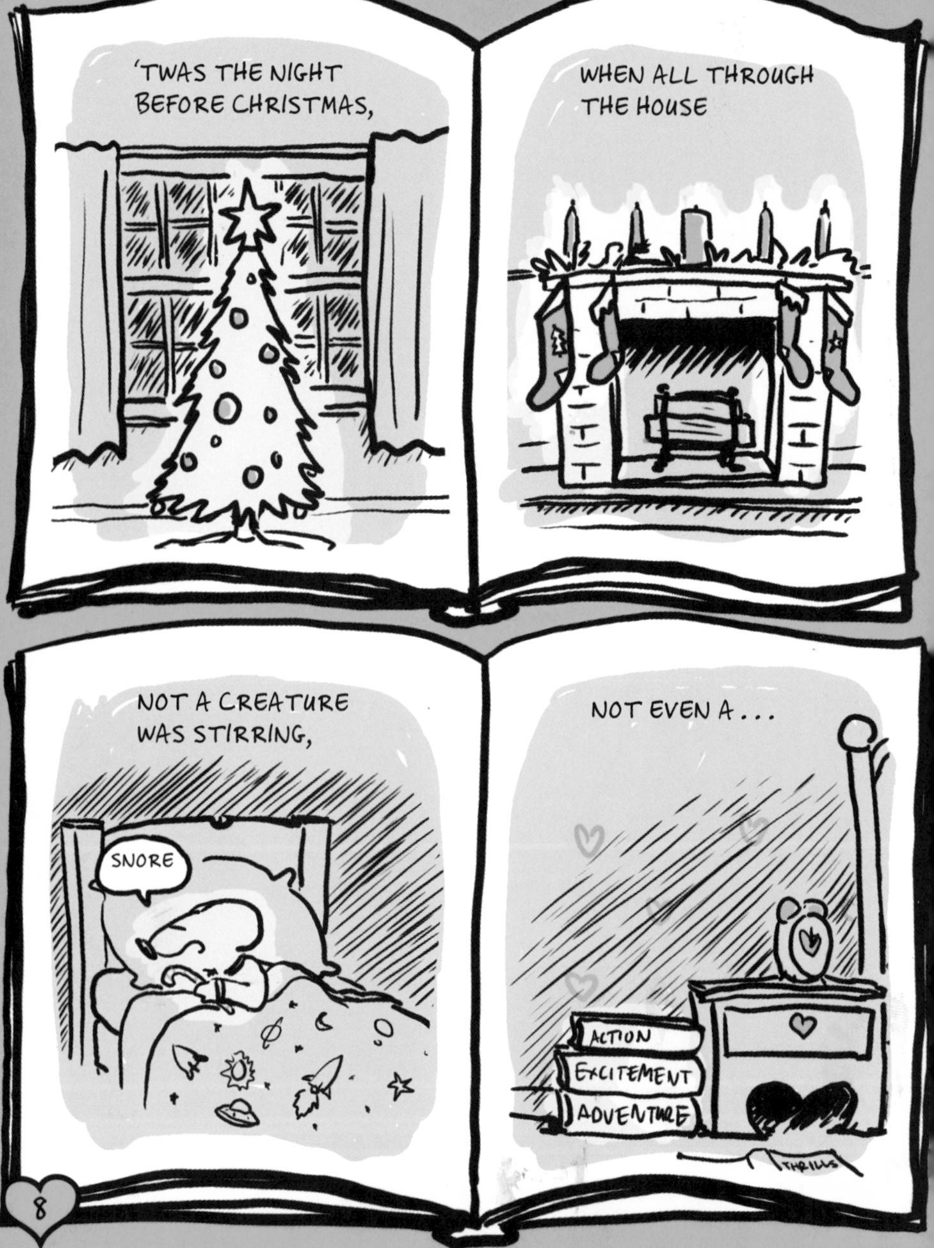
'TWAS THE NIGHT BEFORE CHRISTMAS,
WHEN ALL THROUGH THE HOUSE
NOT A CREATURE WAS STIRRING,
SNORE
NOT EVEN A . . .
ACTION
EXCITEMENT
ADVENTURE
THRILLS

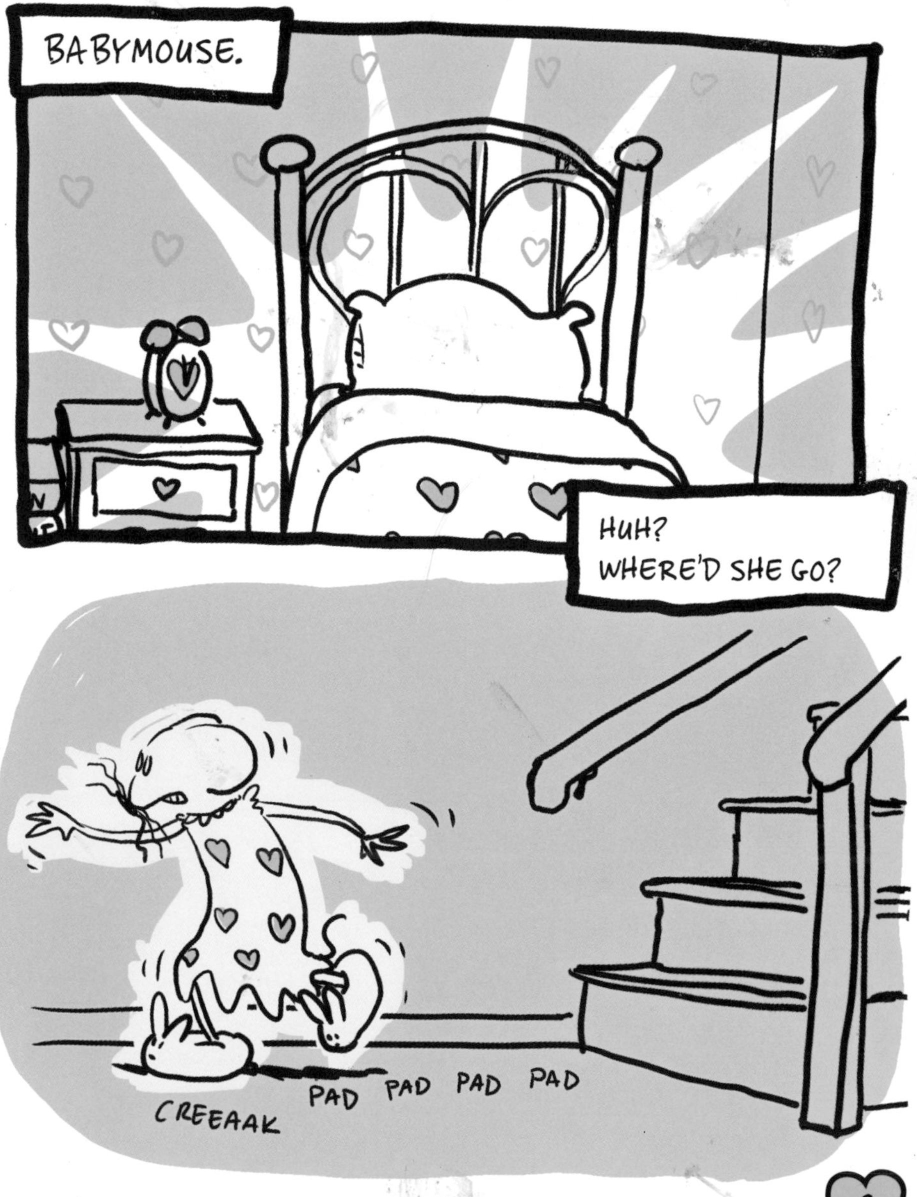

BABYMOUSE.
HUH?
WHERE'D SHE GO?
CREEAAK
PAD PAD PAD PAD

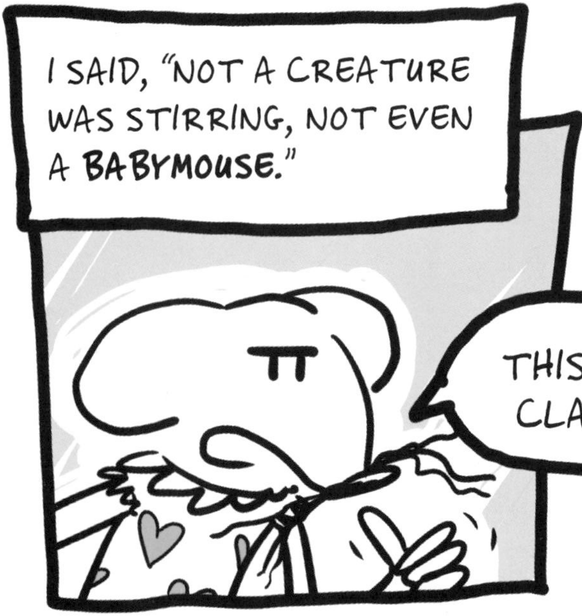
I SAID, "NOT A CREATURE WAS STIRRING, NOT EVEN A **BABYMOUSE.**"
THIS IS **MY** CLASSIC.

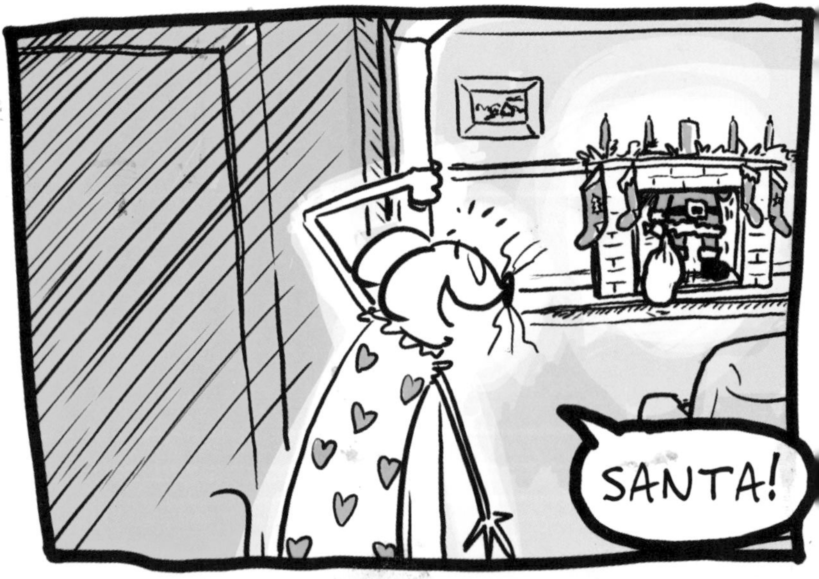
SANTA!

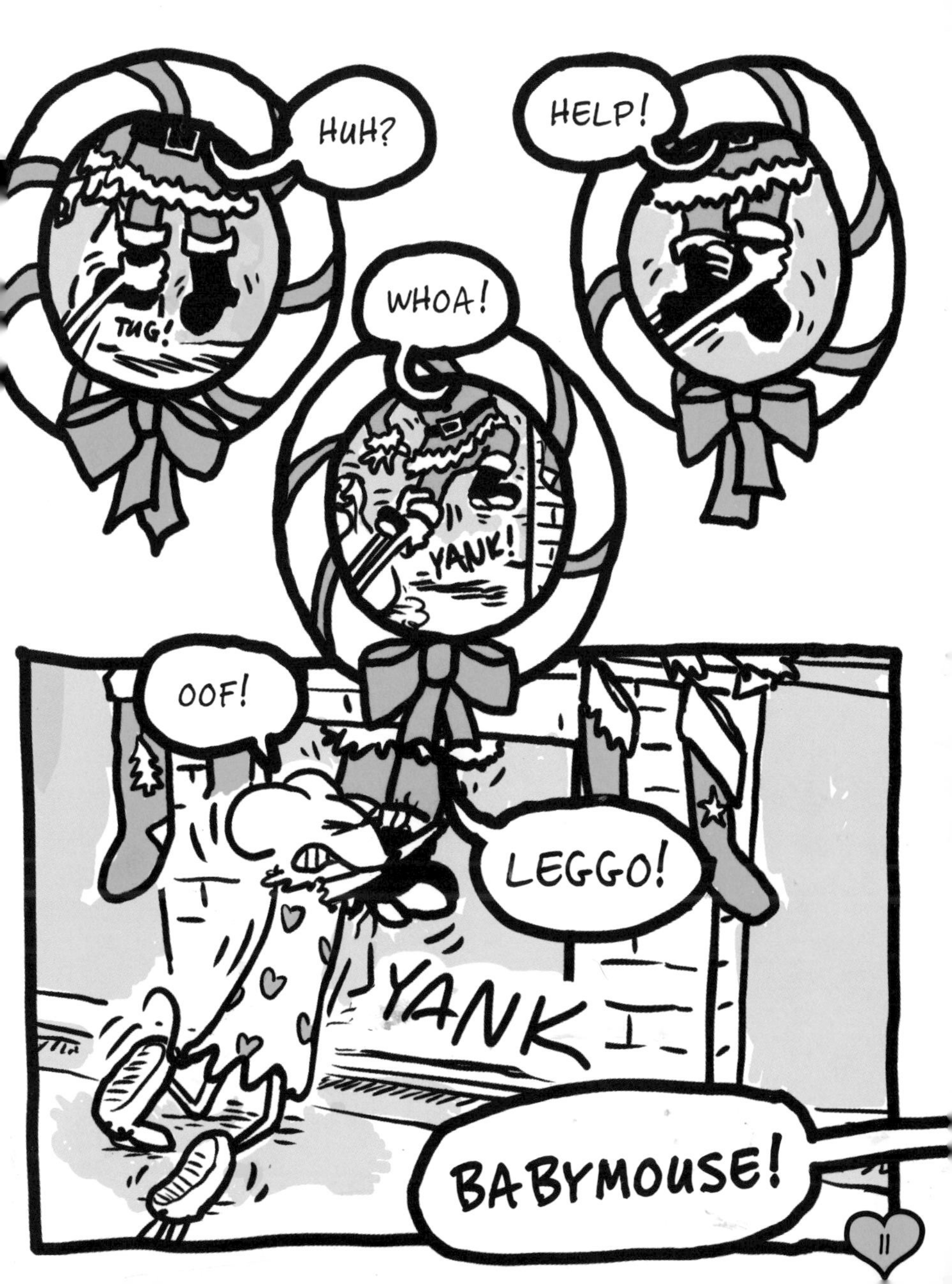
HUH?
TUG!
HELP!
WHOA!
YANK!
OOF!
LEGGO!
YANK
BABYMOUSE!
11

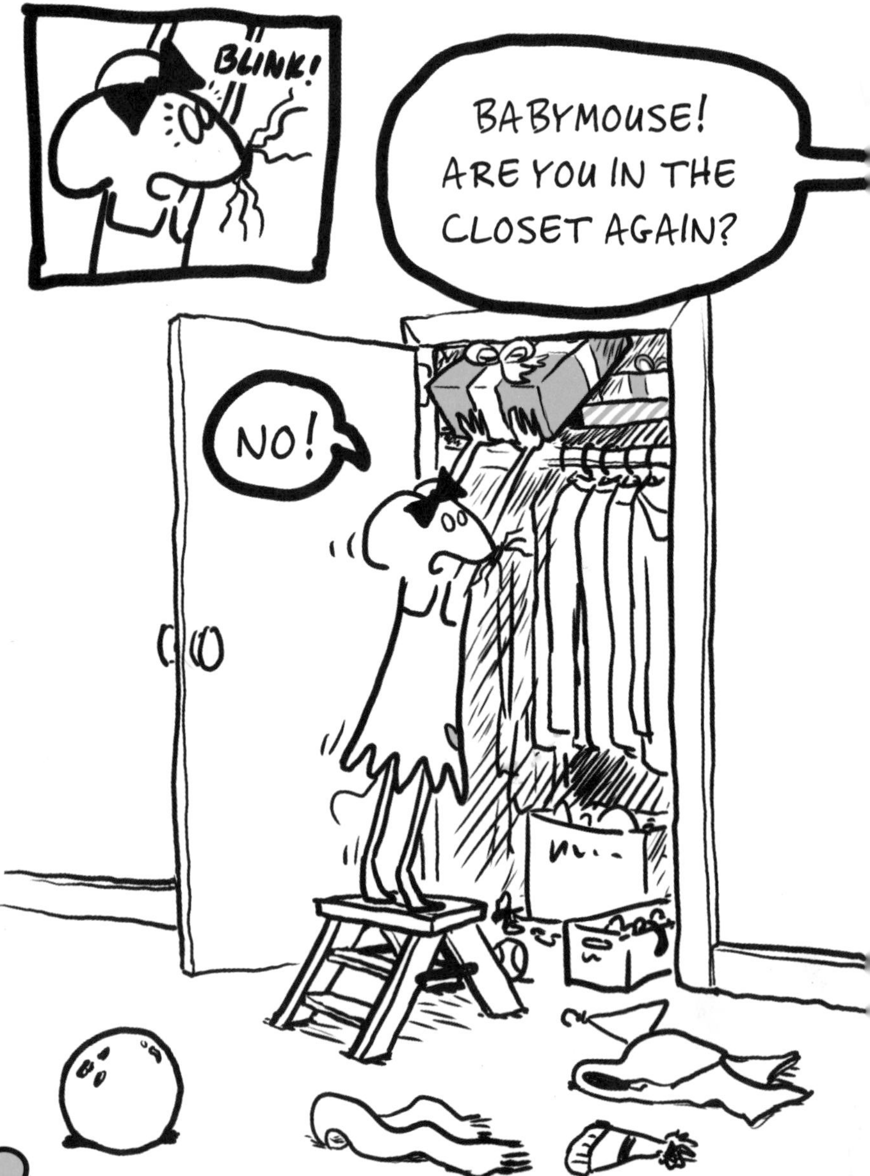
BLINK!
BABYMOUSE! ARE YOU IN THE CLOSET AGAIN?
NO!

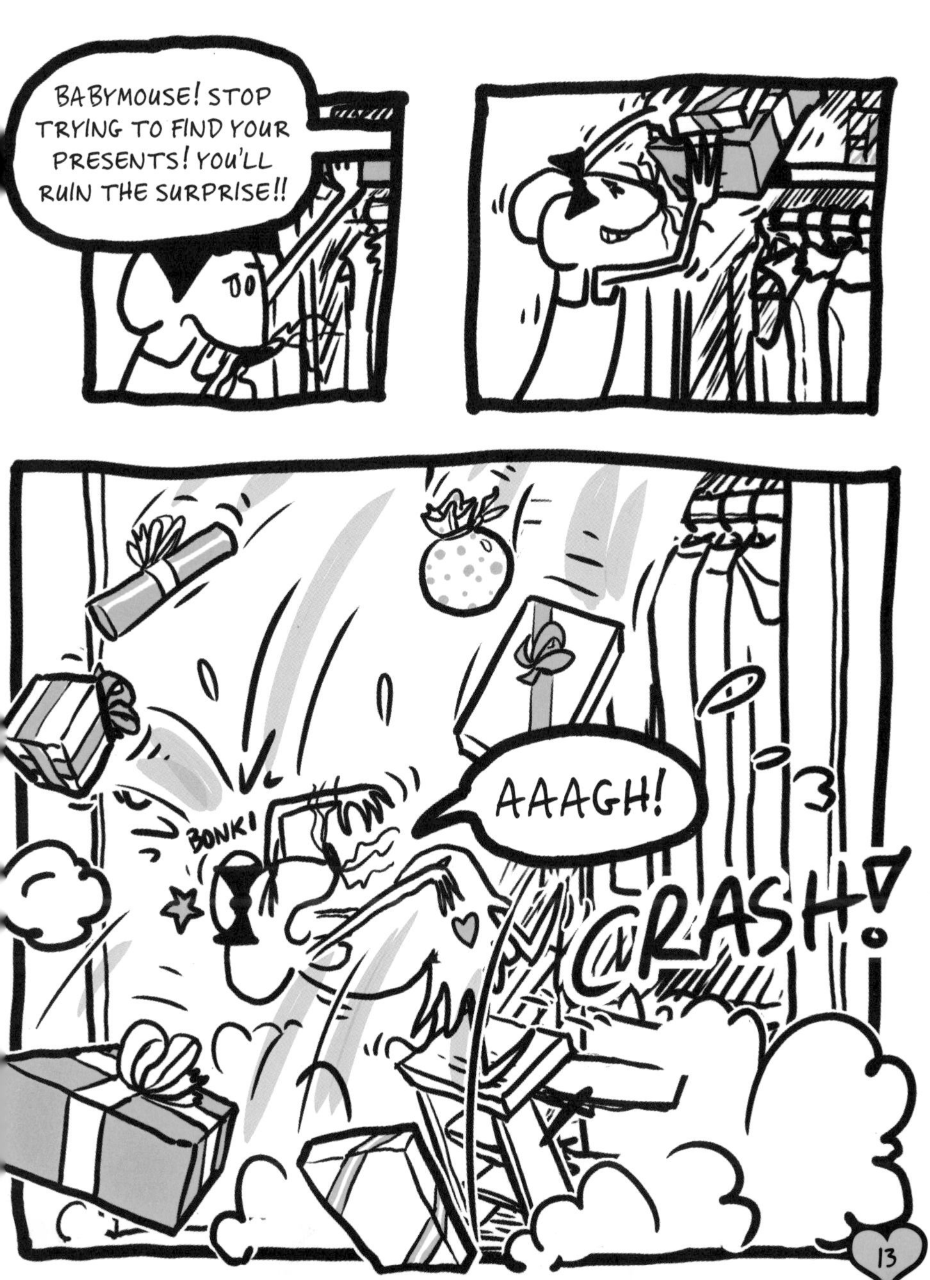
BABYMOUSE! STOP TRYING TO FIND YOUR PRESENTS! YOU'LL RUIN THE SURPRISE!!
BONK!
AAAGH!
CRASH!

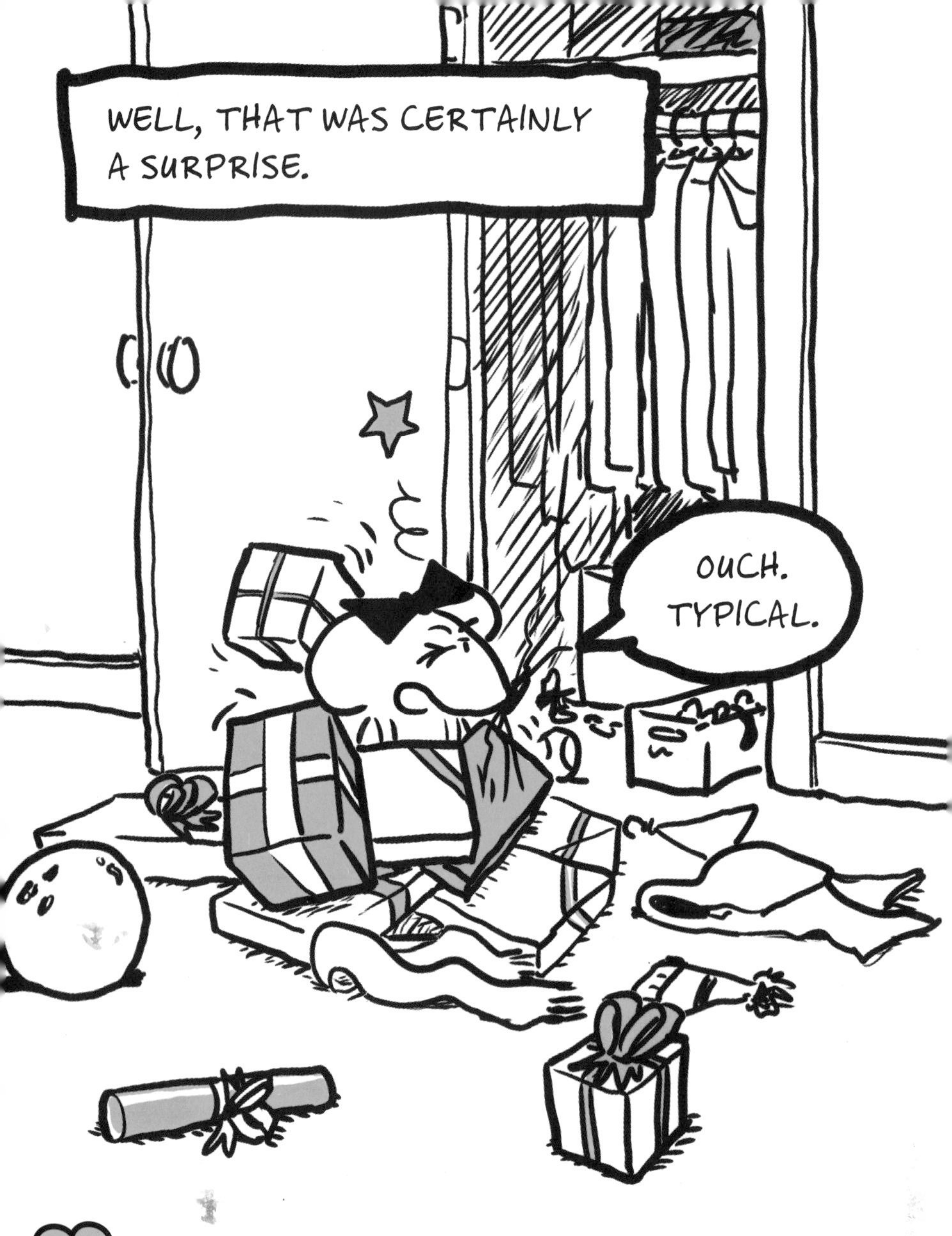
WELL, THAT WAS CERTAINLY A SURPRISE.
OUCH. TYPICAL.

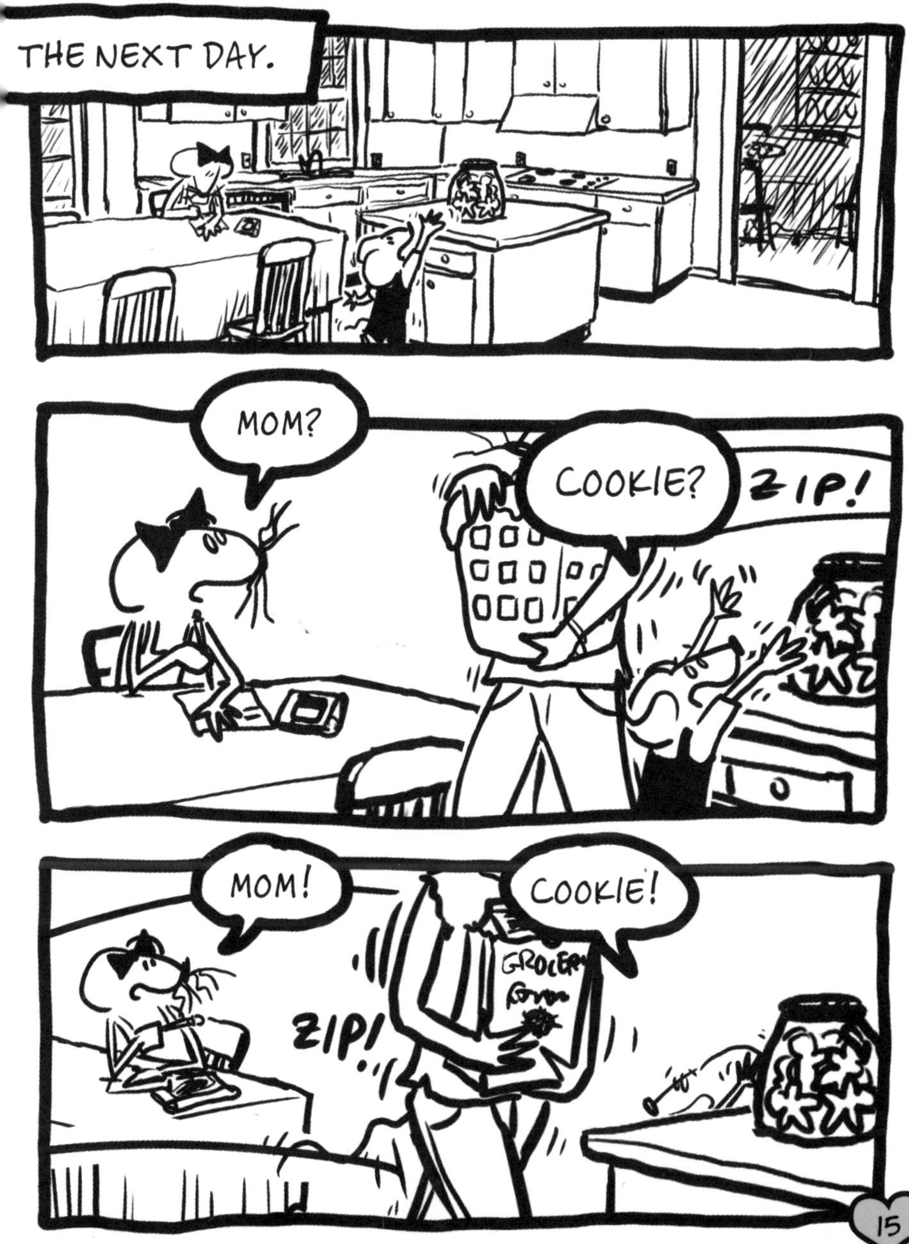
THE NEXT DAY.
MOM?
COOKIE?
ZIP!
MOM!
COOKIE!
ZIP!

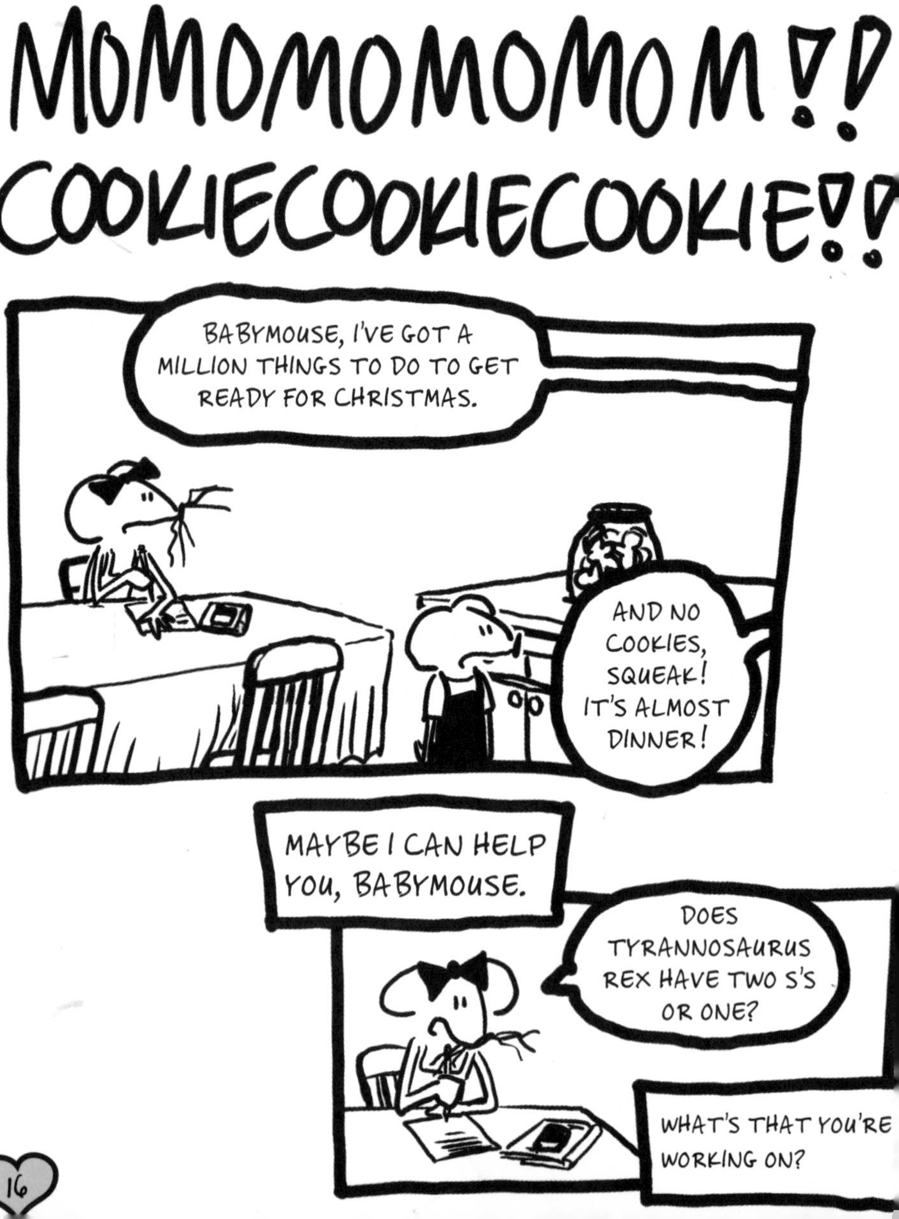
MOMOMOMOMOMOM!!
COOKIECOOKIECOOKIE!!
BABYMOUSE, I'VE GOT A MILLION THINGS TO DO TO GET READY FOR CHRISTMAS.
AND NO COOKIES, SQUEAK! IT'S ALMOST DINNER!
MAYBE I CAN HELP YOU, BABYMOUSE.
DOES TYRANNOSAURUS REX HAVE TWO S'S OR ONE?
WHAT'S THAT YOU'RE WORKING ON?

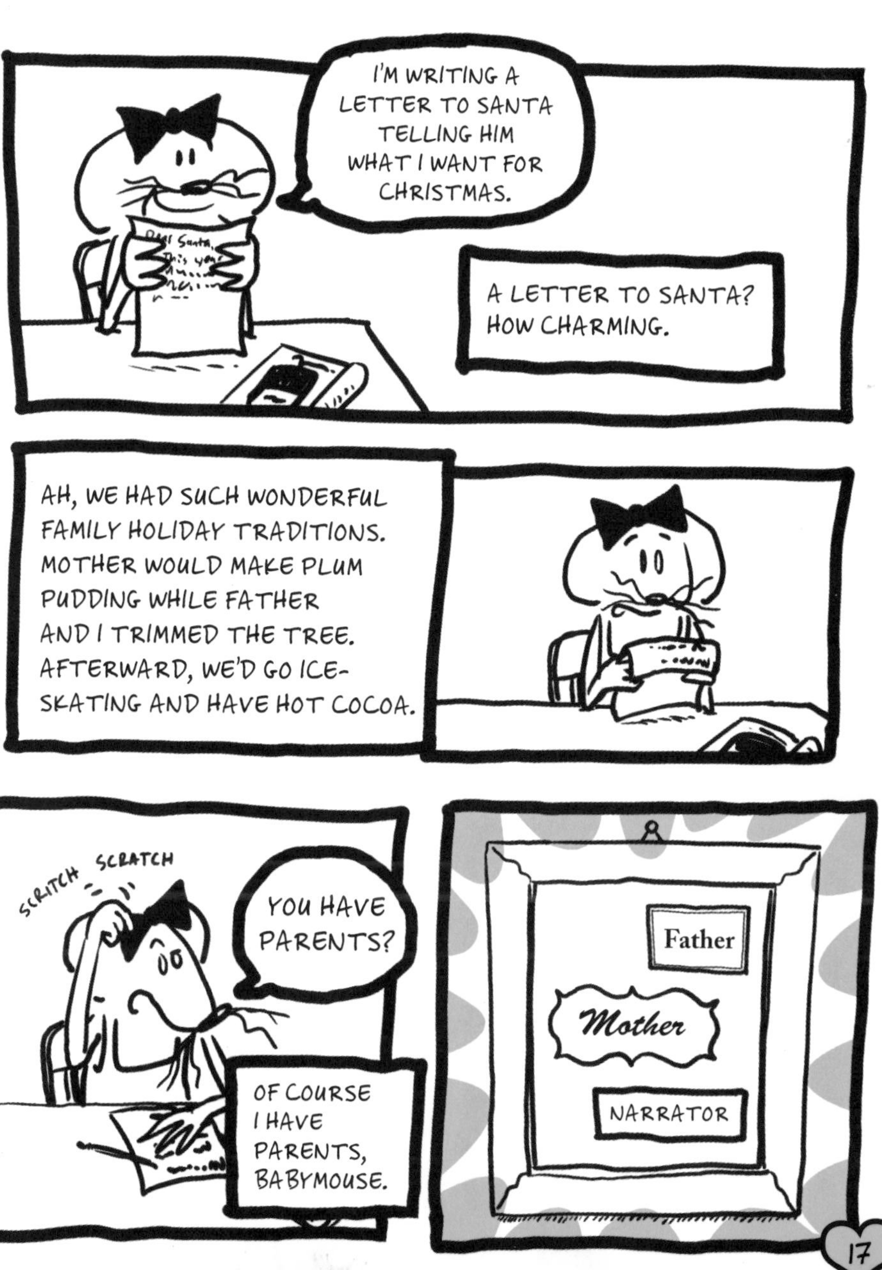
I'M WRITING A LETTER TO SANTA TELLING HIM WHAT I WANT FOR CHRISTMAS.
A LETTER TO SANTA? HOW CHARMING.
AH, WE HAD SUCH WONDERFUL FAMILY HOLIDAY TRADITIONS. MOTHER WOULD MAKE PLUM PUDDING WHILE FATHER AND I TRIMMED THE TREE. AFTERWARD, WE'D GO ICE-SKATING AND HAVE HOT COCOA.
SCRITCH SCRATCH
YOU HAVE PARENTS?
OF COURSE I HAVE PARENTS, BABYMOUSE.
Father
Mother
NARRATOR

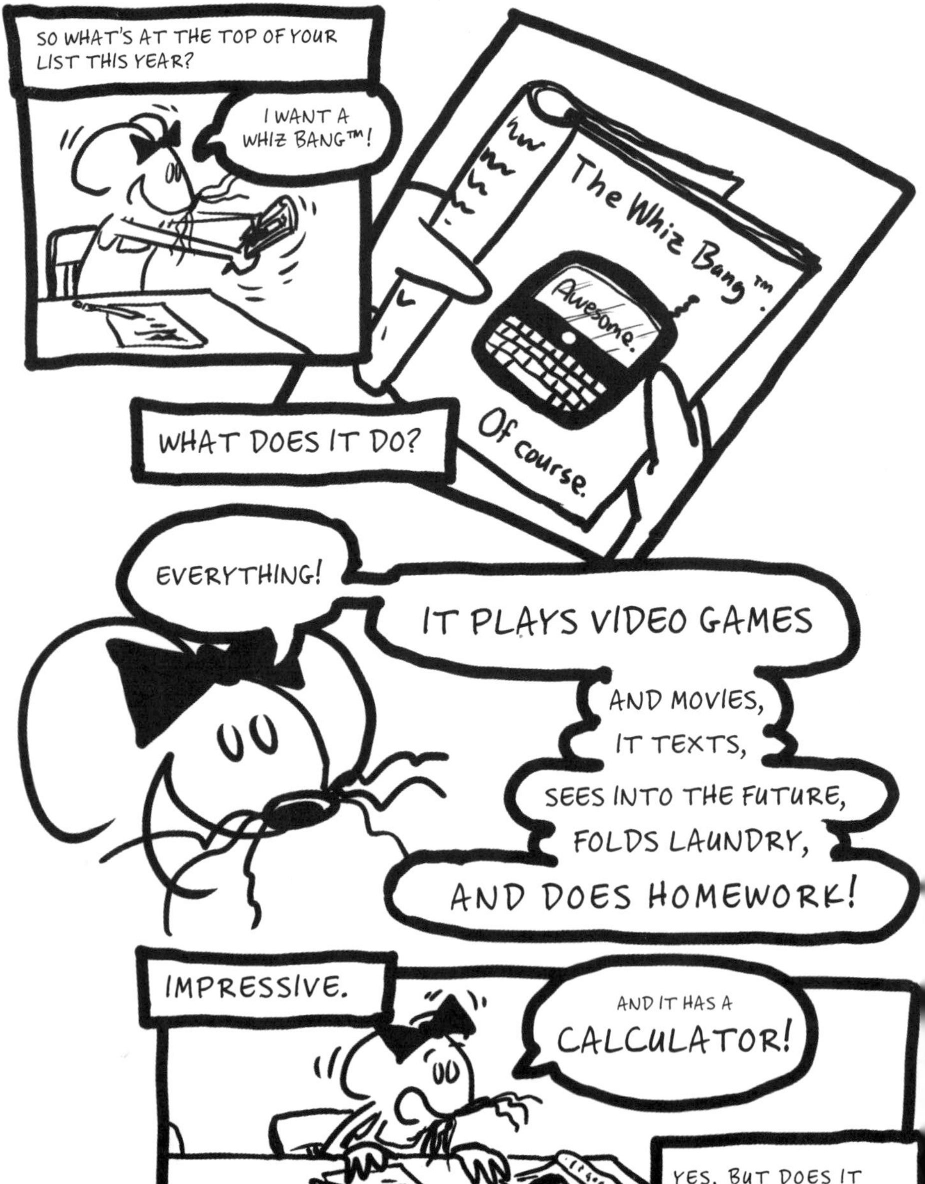
SO WHAT'S AT THE TOP OF YOUR LIST THIS YEAR?
I WANT A WHIZ BANG™!
The Whiz Bang™.
Awesome.
Of course.
WHAT DOES IT DO?
EVERYTHING!
IT PLAYS VIDEO GAMES
AND MOVIES,
IT TEXTS,
SEES INTO THE FUTURE,
FOLDS LAUNDRY,
AND DOES HOMEWORK!
IMPRESSIVE.
AND IT HAS A CALCULATOR!
YES, BUT DOES IT STRAIGHTEN WHISKERS?

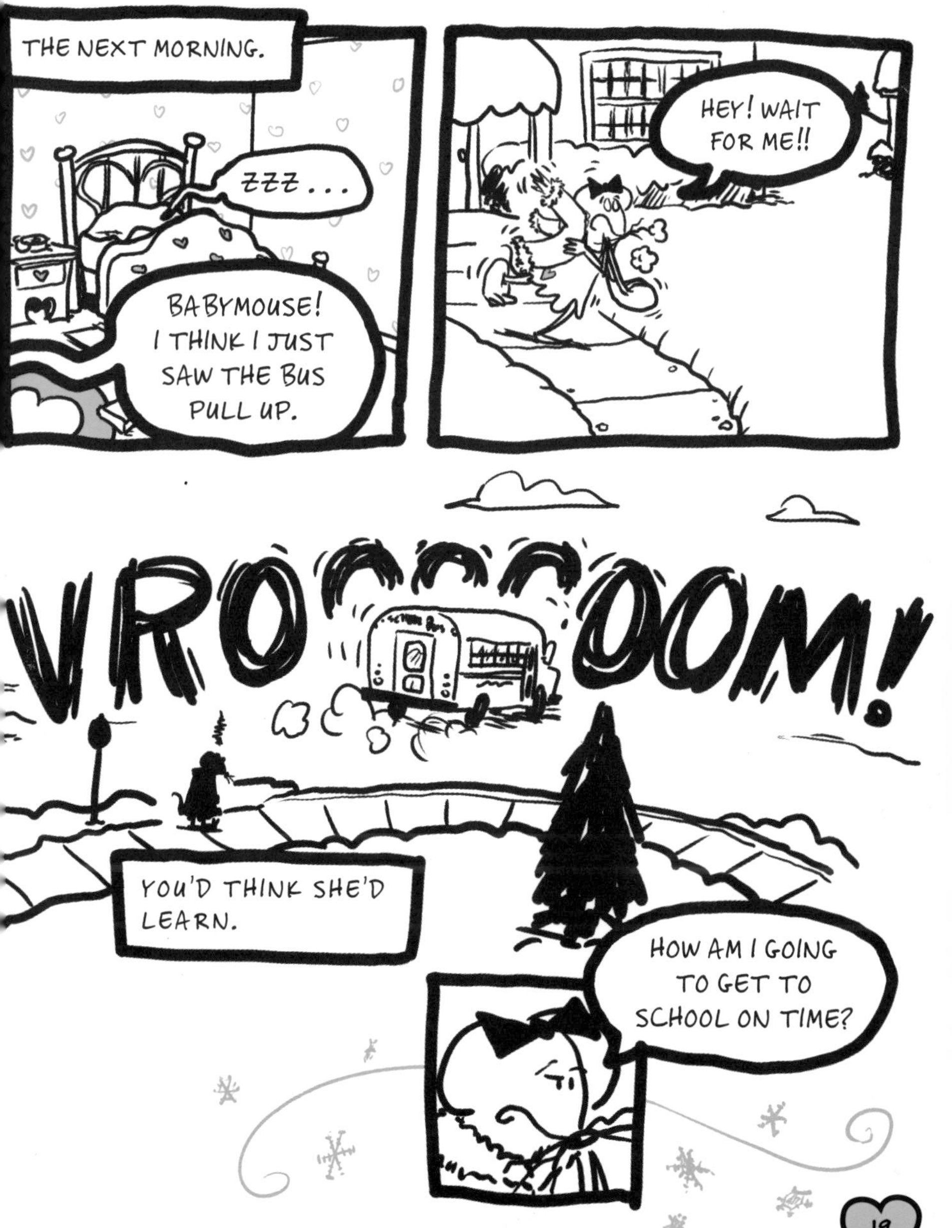
THE NEXT MORNING.
ZZZ . . .
BABYMOUSE! I THINK I JUST SAW THE BUS PULL UP.
HEY! WAIT FOR ME!!
VROOOOOOM!
YOU'D THINK SHE'D LEARN.
HOW AM I GOING TO GET TO SCHOOL ON TIME?

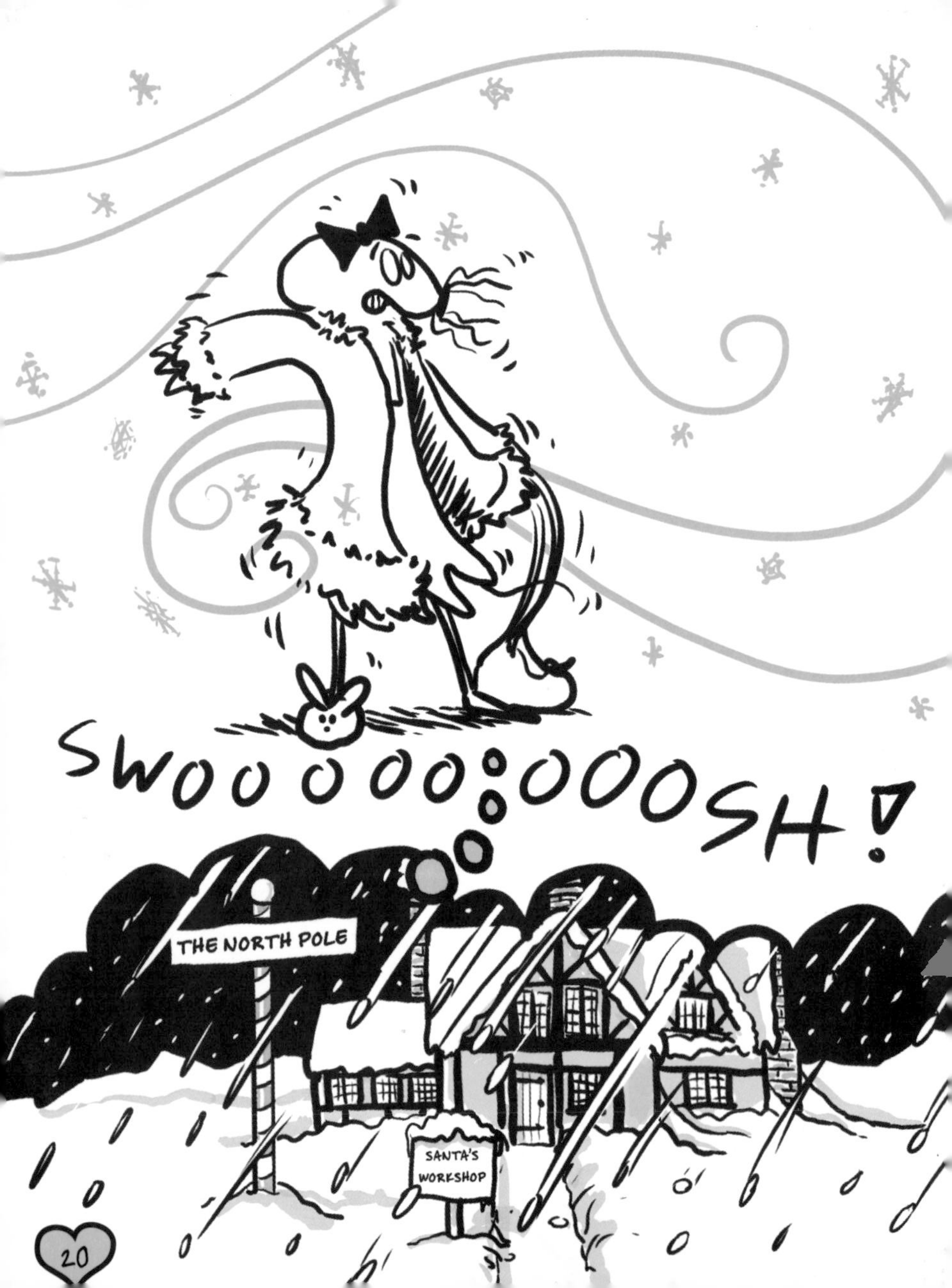
SWOOOOOO:OOOOSH!
THE NORTH POLE
SANTA'S WORKSHOP

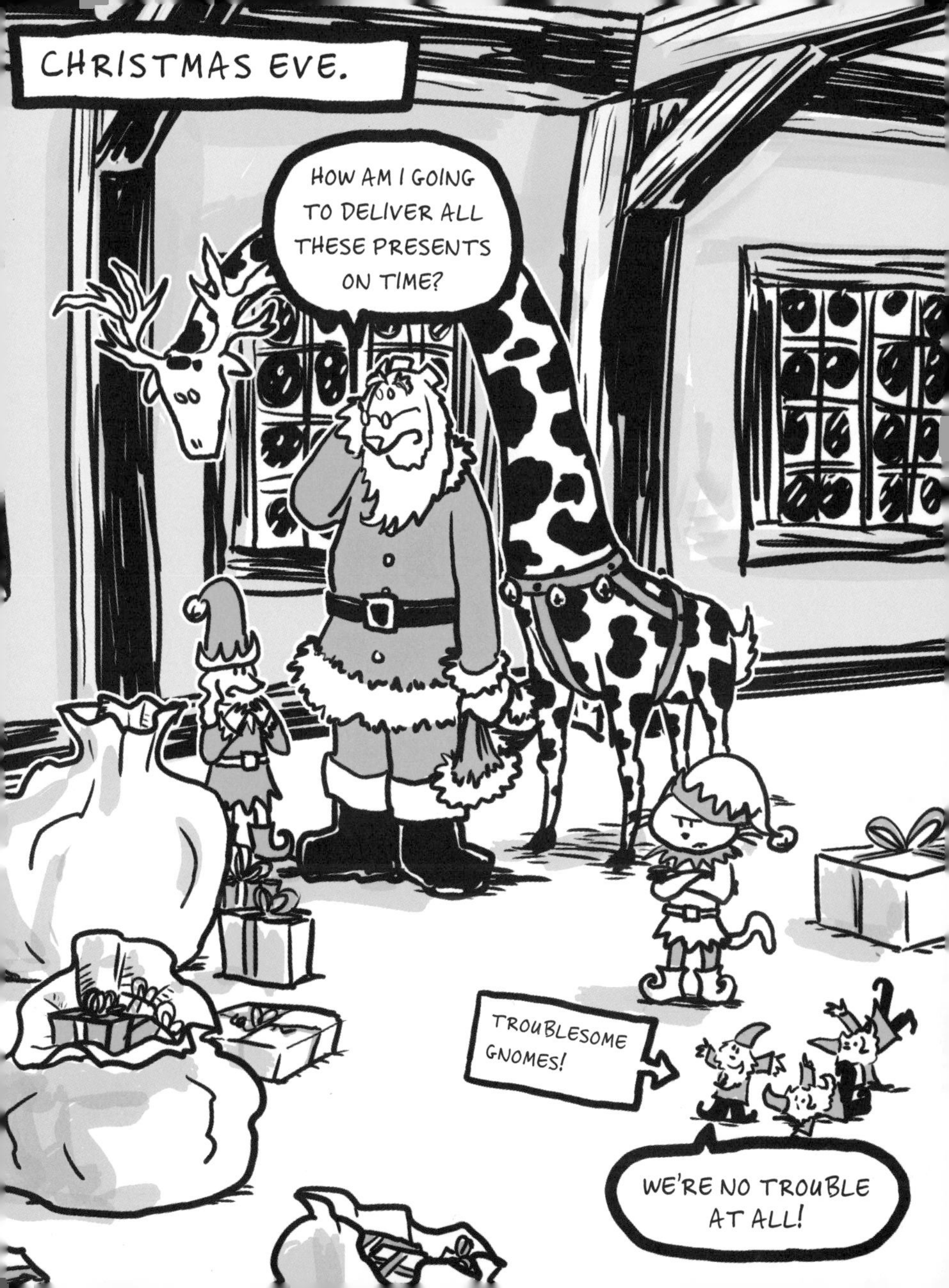
CHRISTMAS EVE.
HOW AM I GOING TO DELIVER ALL THESE PRESENTS ON TIME?
TROUBLESOME GNOMES!
WE'RE NO TROUBLE AT ALL!

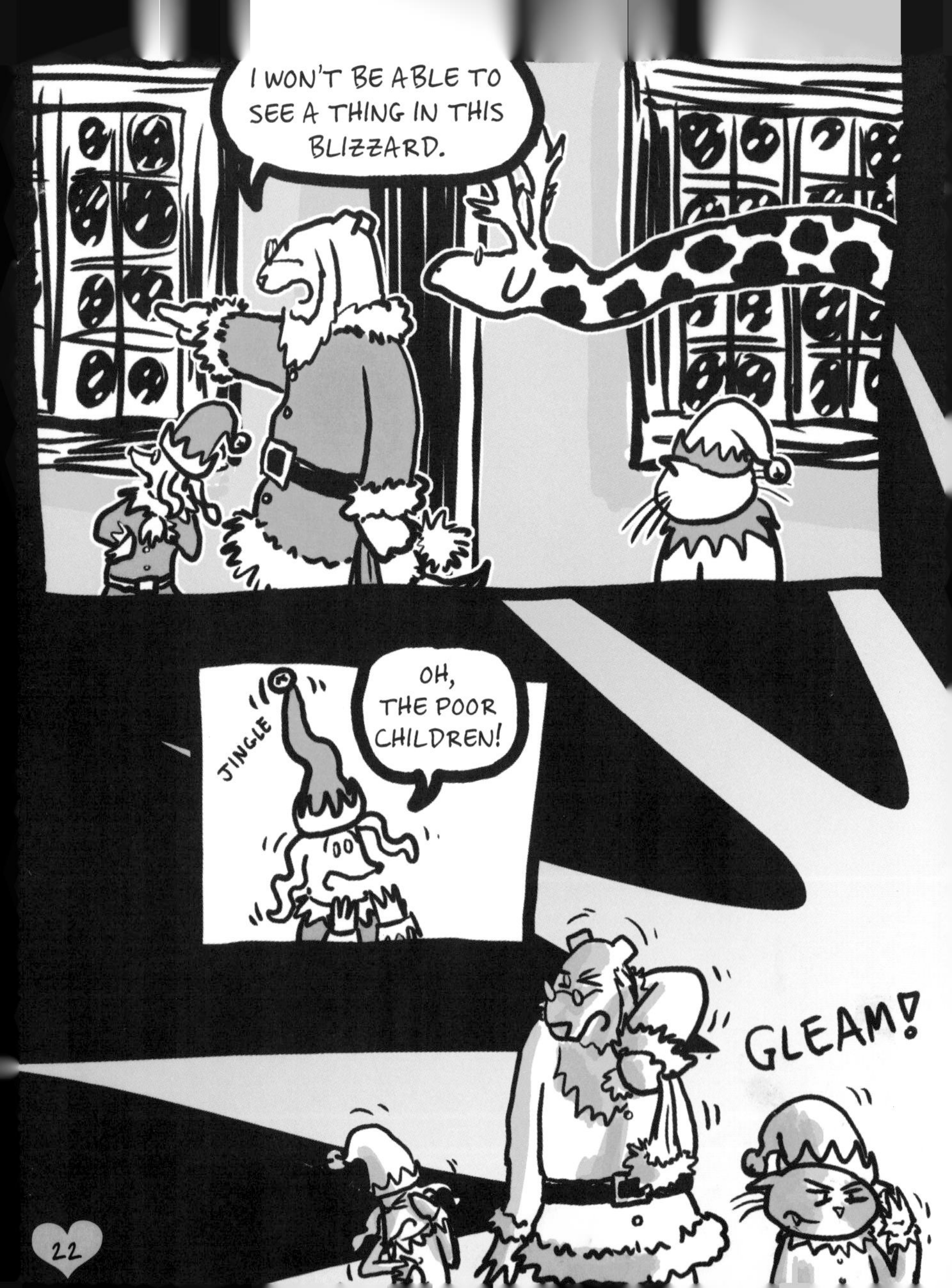
I WON'T BE ABLE TO SEE A THING IN THIS BLIZZARD.
JINGLE
OH, THE POOR CHILDREN!
GLEAM!

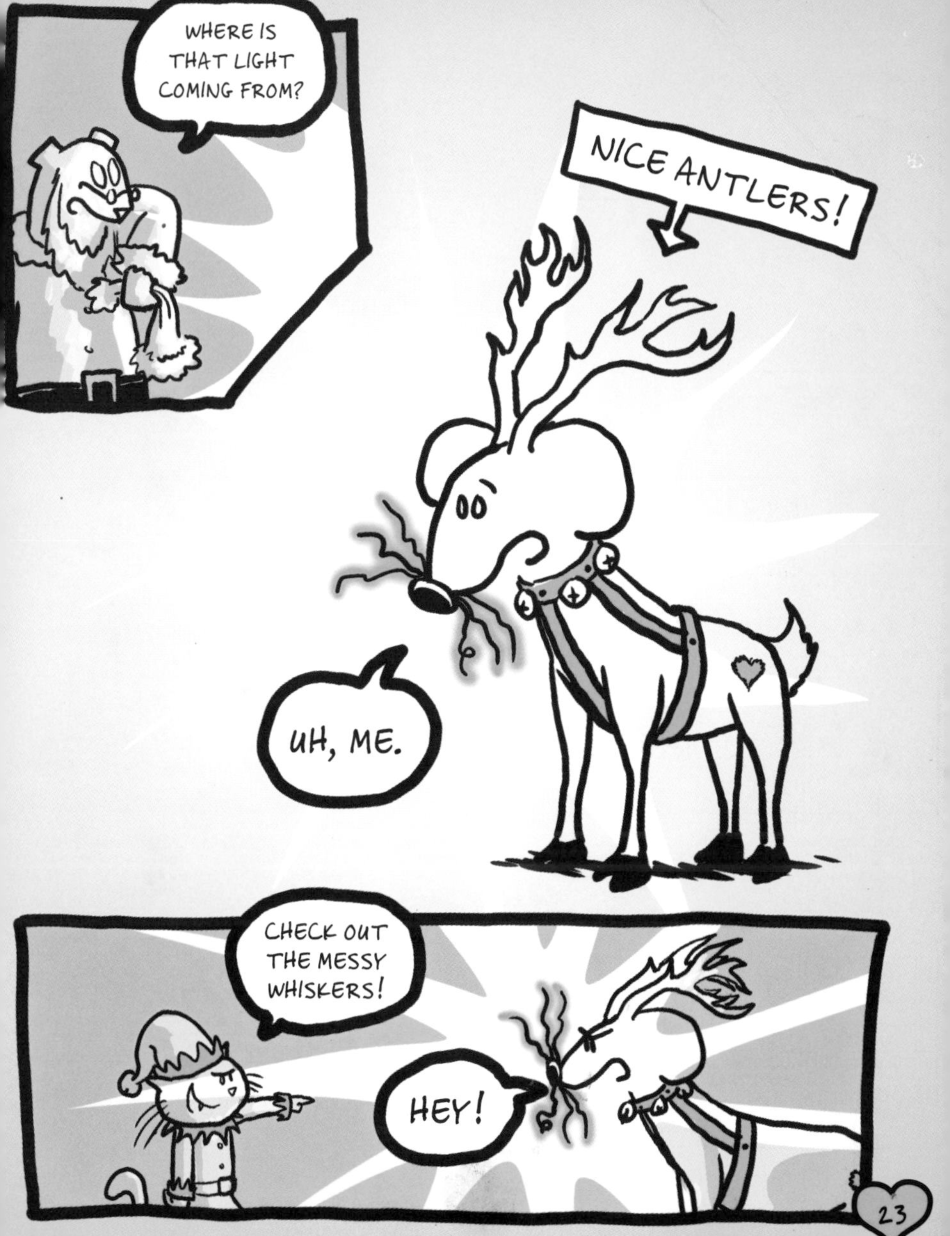
WHERE IS THAT LIGHT COMING FROM?
NICE ANTLERS!
UH, ME.
CHECK OUT THE MESSY WHISKERS!
HEY!

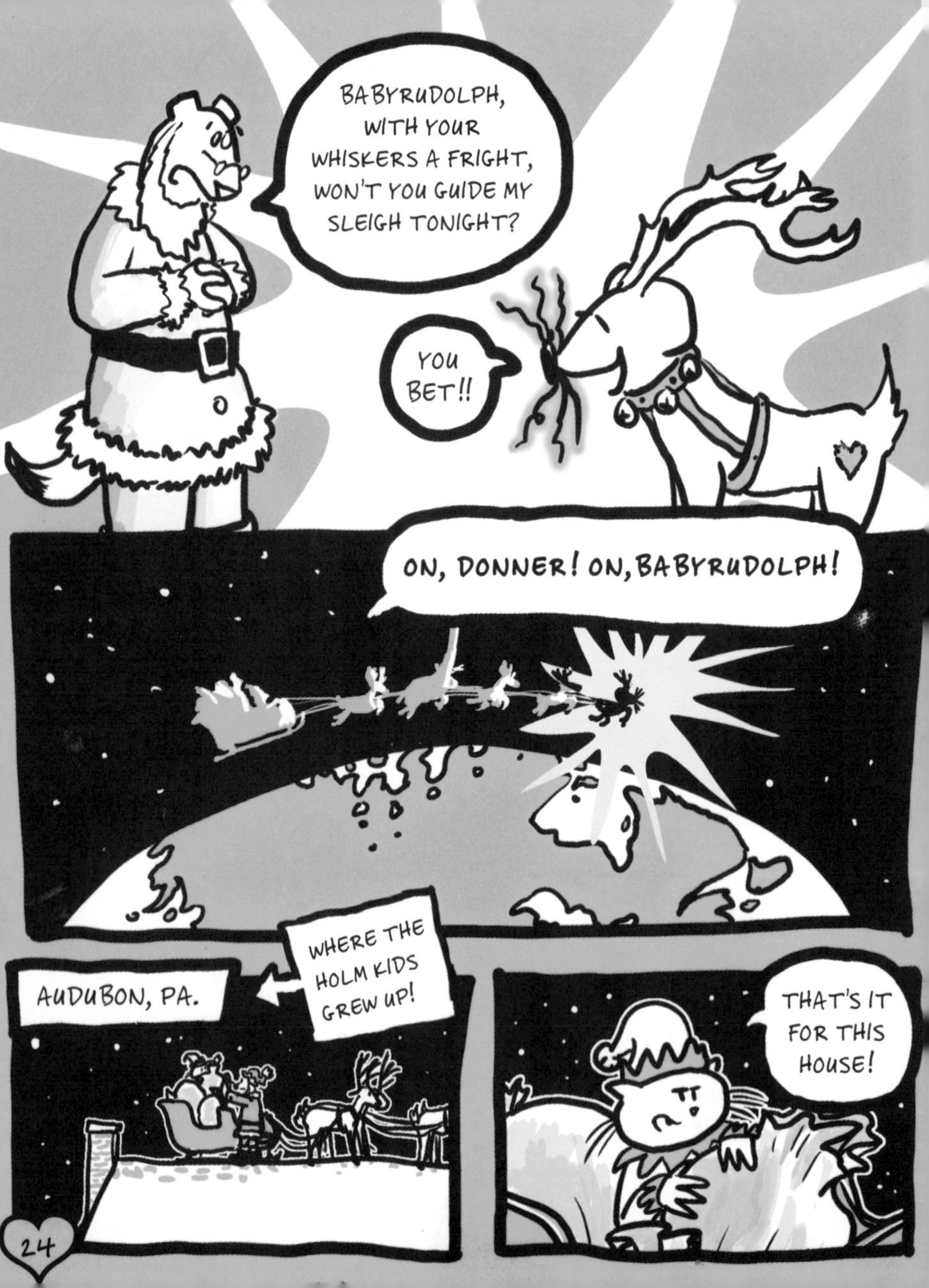
BABYRUDOLPH, WITH YOUR WHISKERS A FRIGHT, WON'T YOU GUIDE MY SLEIGH TONIGHT?
YOU BET!!
ON, DONNER! ON, BABYRUDOLPH!
AUDUBON, PA.
WHERE THE HOLM KIDS GREW UP!
THAT'S IT FOR THIS HOUSE!

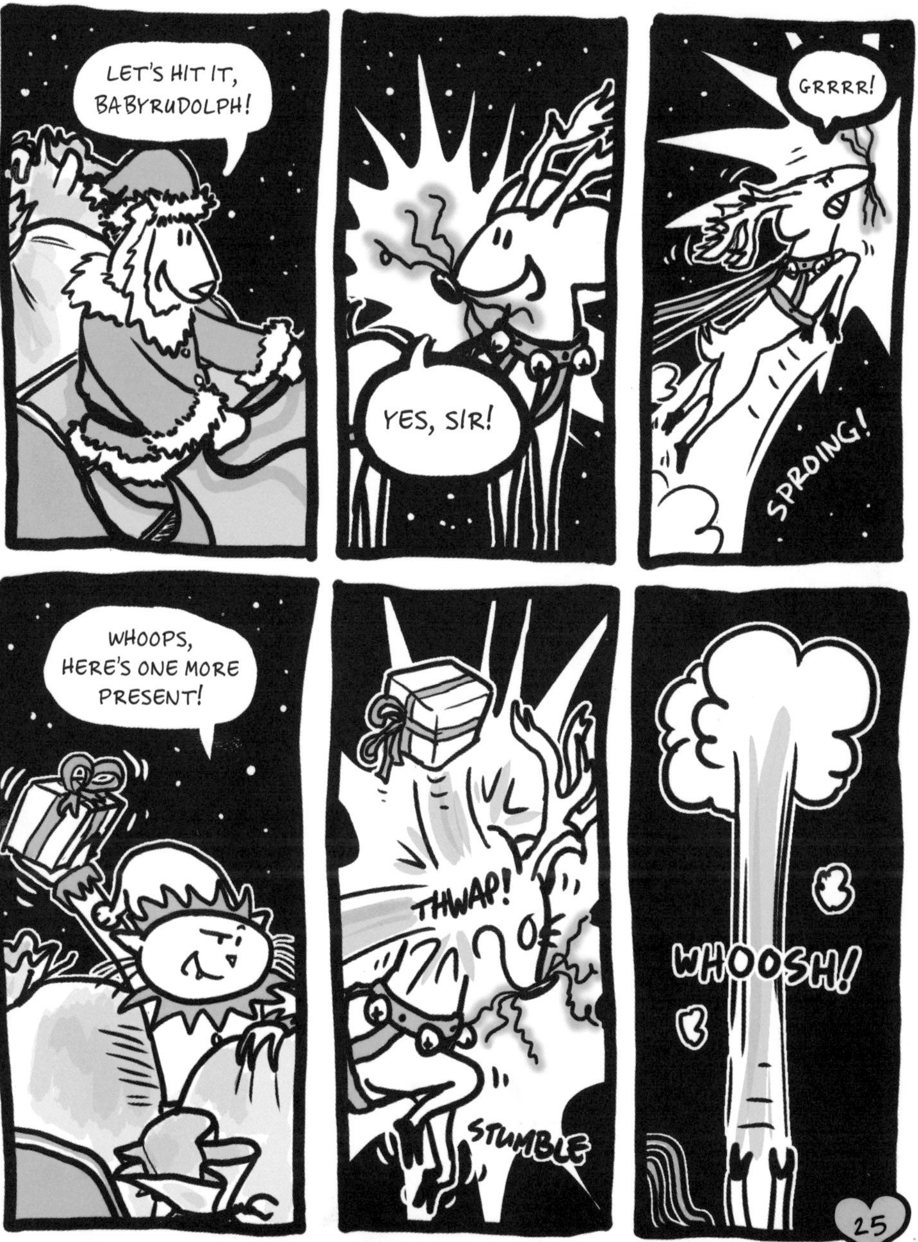
LET'S HIT IT, BABYRUDOLPH!
YES, SIR!
GRRRR!
SPROING!
WHOOPS, HERE'S ONE MORE PRESENT!
THWAP!
STUMBLE
WHOOSH!

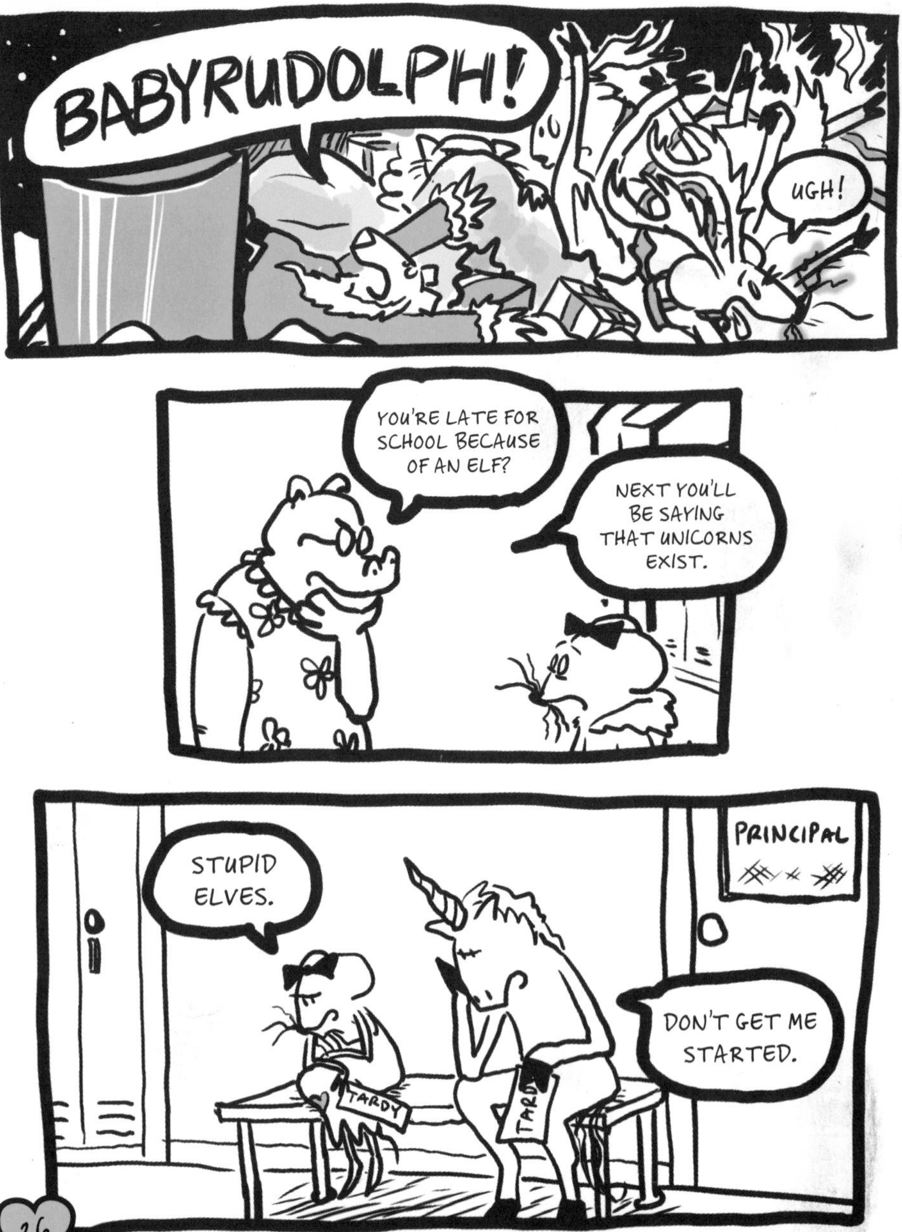
BABYRUDOLPH!
UGH!
YOU'RE LATE FOR SCHOOL BECAUSE OF AN ELF?
NEXT YOU'LL BE SAYING THAT UNICORNS EXIST.
STUPID ELVES.
PRINCIPAL
DON'T GET ME STARTED.
TARDY
TARDY

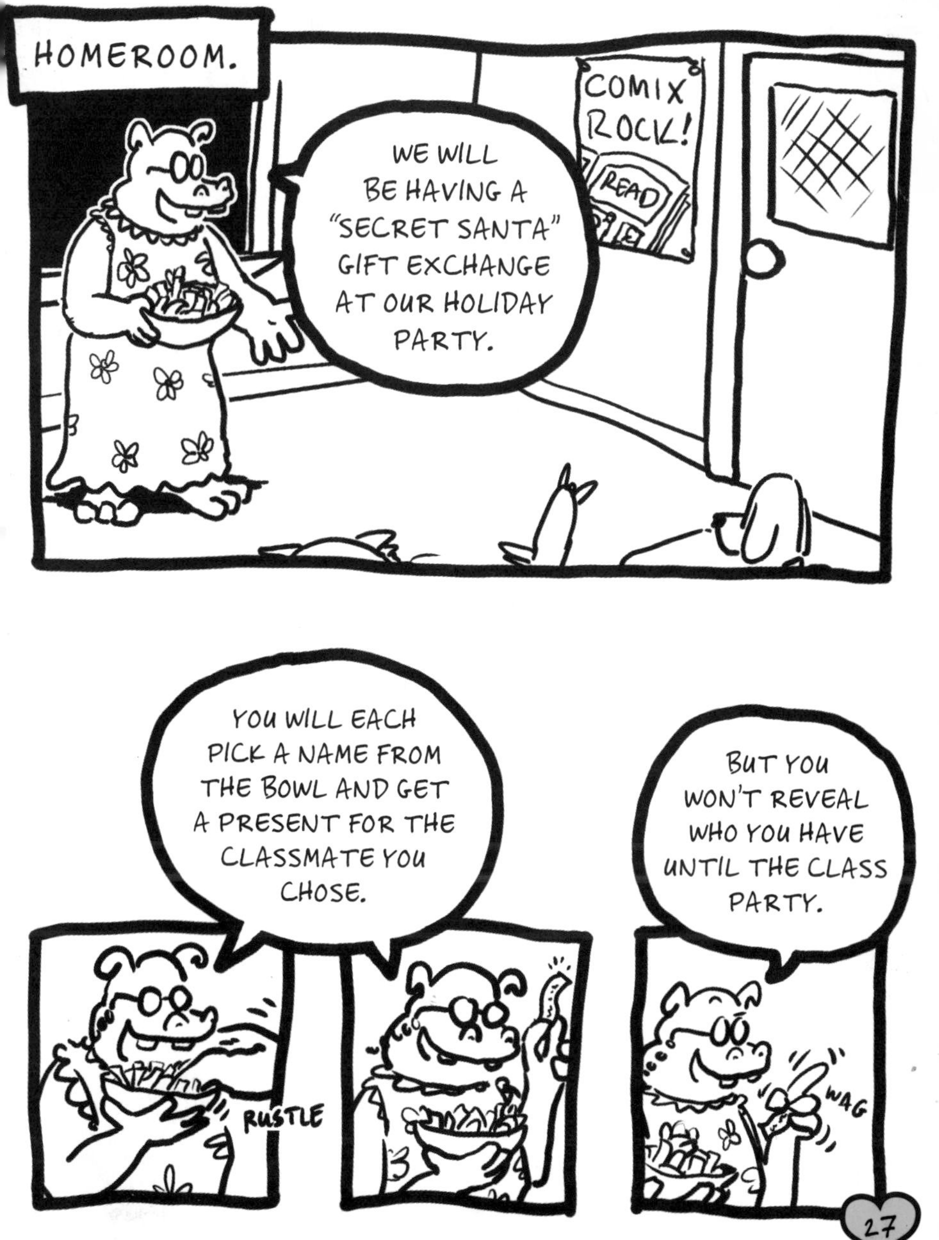
HOMEROOM.
COMIX ROCK!
READ
WE WILL BE HAVING A "SECRET SANTA" GIFT EXCHANGE AT OUR HOLIDAY PARTY.
YOU WILL EACH PICK A NAME FROM THE BOWL AND GET A PRESENT FOR THE CLASSMATE YOU CHOSE.
RUSTLE
BUT YOU WON'T REVEAL WHO YOU HAVE UNTIL THE CLASS PARTY.
WAG

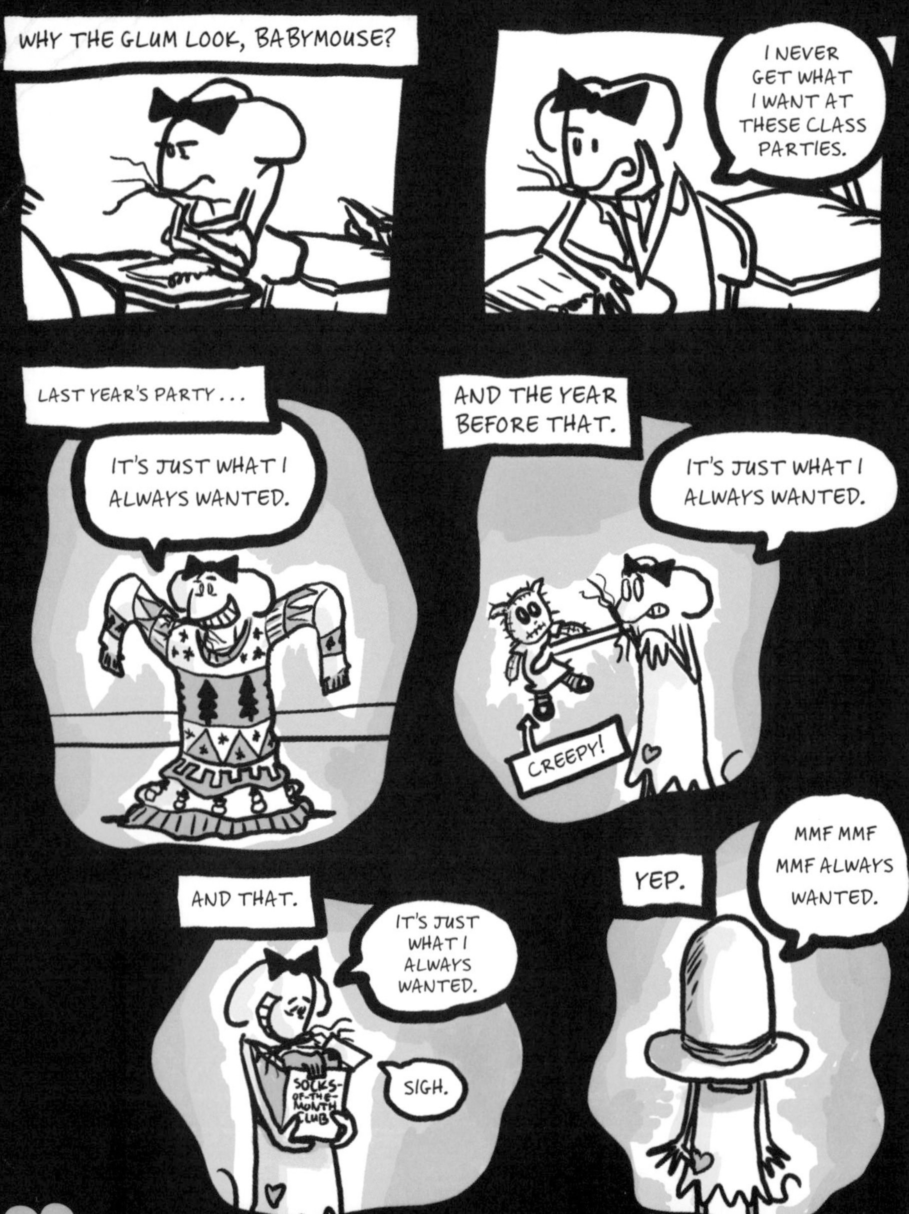
WHY THE GLUM LOOK, BABYMOUSE?
I NEVER GET WHAT I WANT AT THESE CLASS PARTIES.
LAST YEAR'S PARTY . . .
IT'S JUST WHAT I ALWAYS WANTED.
AND THE YEAR BEFORE THAT.
IT'S JUST WHAT I ALWAYS WANTED.
CREEPY!
AND THAT.
IT'S JUST WHAT I ALWAYS WANTED.
SOCKS-OF-THE-MONTH CLUB
SIGH.
YEP.
MMF MMF MMF ALWAYS WANTED.

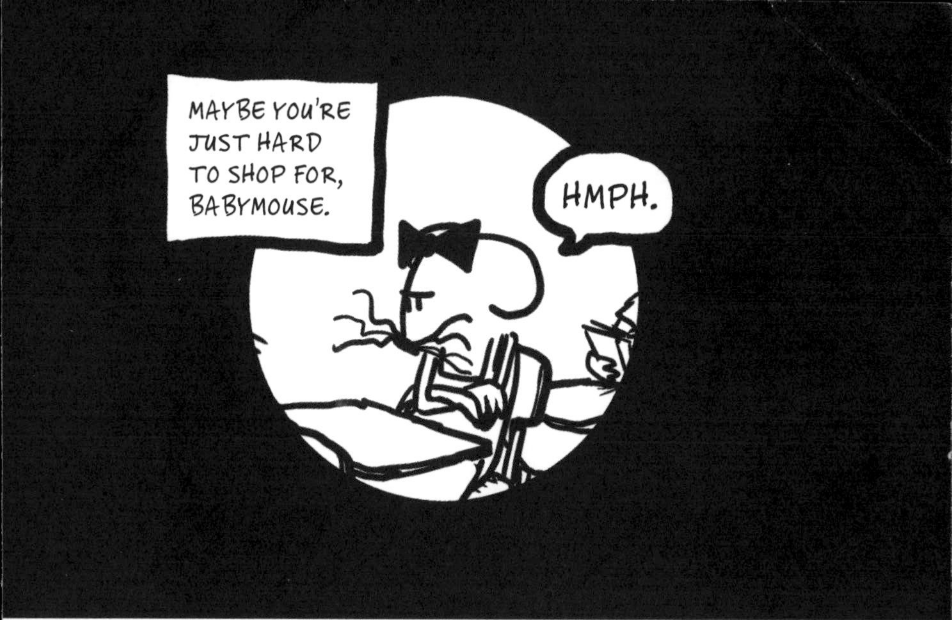
MAYBE YOU'RE JUST HARD TO SHOP FOR, BABYMOUSE.
HMPH.

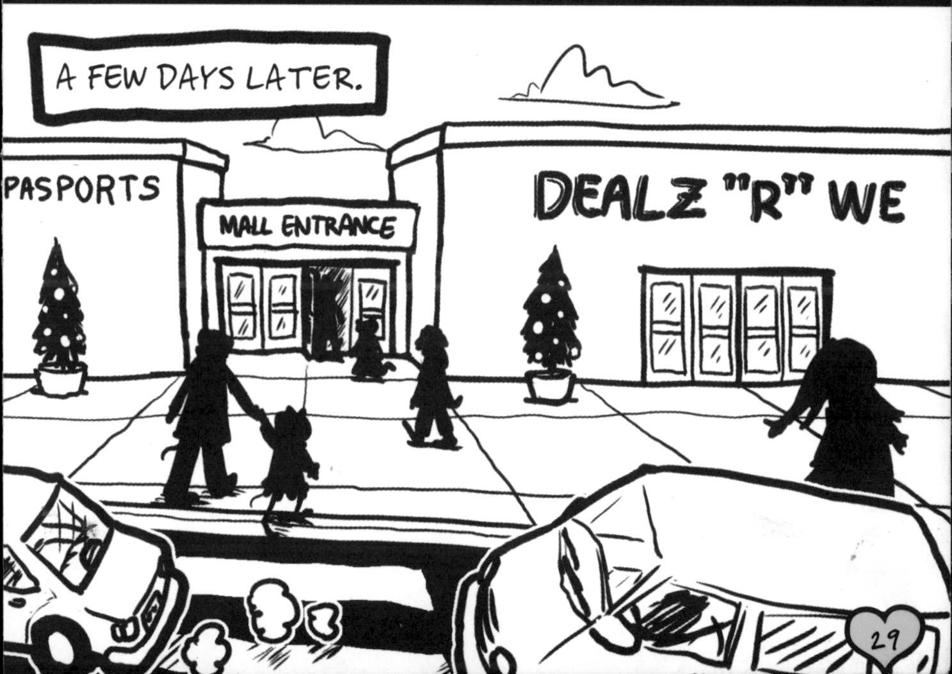
A FEW DAYS LATER.
PASPORTS
MALL ENTRANCE
DEALZ "R" WE

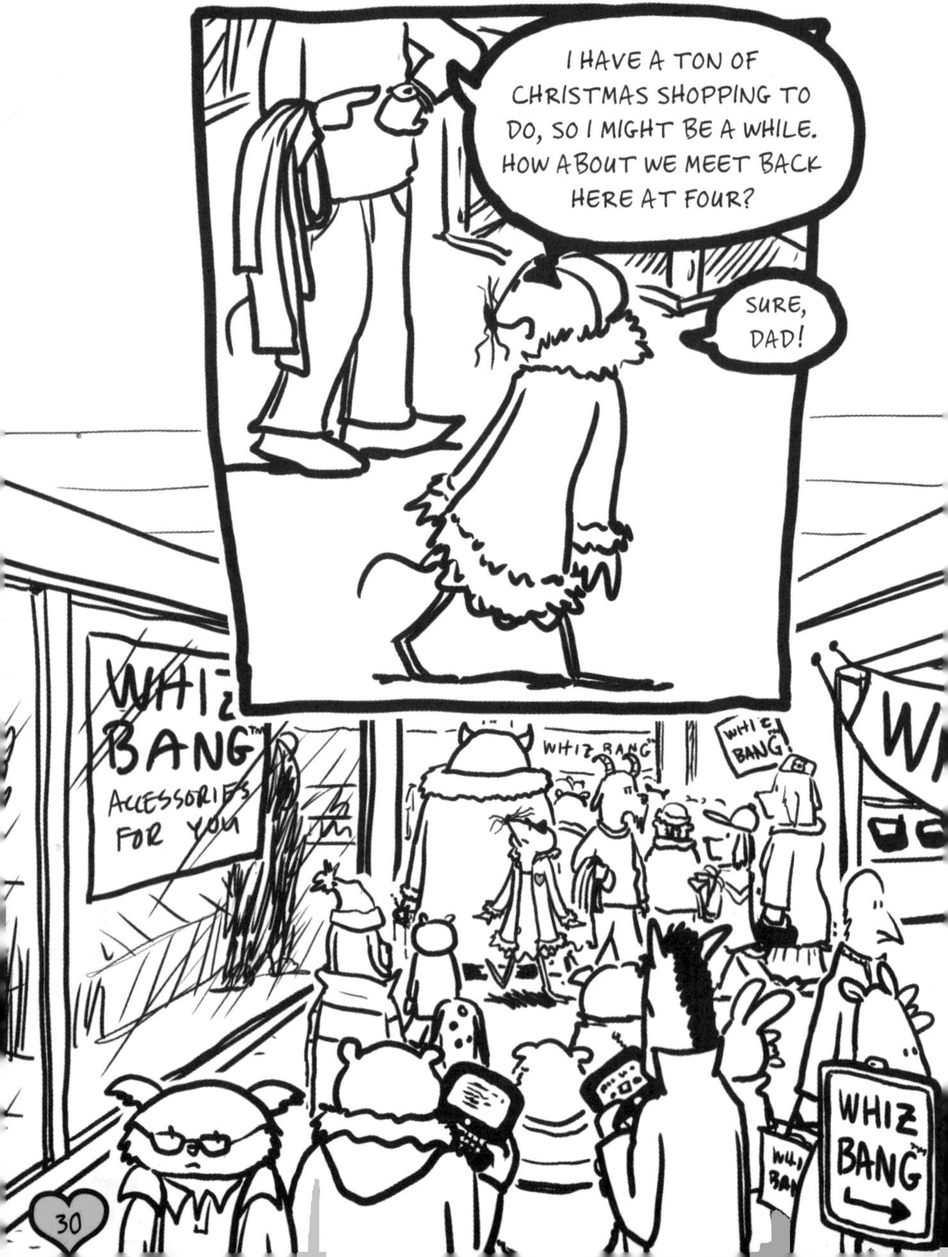
I HAVE A TON OF CHRISTMAS SHOPPING TO DO, SO I MIGHT BE A WHILE. HOW ABOUT WE MEET BACK HERE AT FOUR?
SURE, DAD!
WHIZ BANG™ ACCESSORIES FOR YOU
WHIZ BANG™
WHIZ BANG
WHIZ BANG™

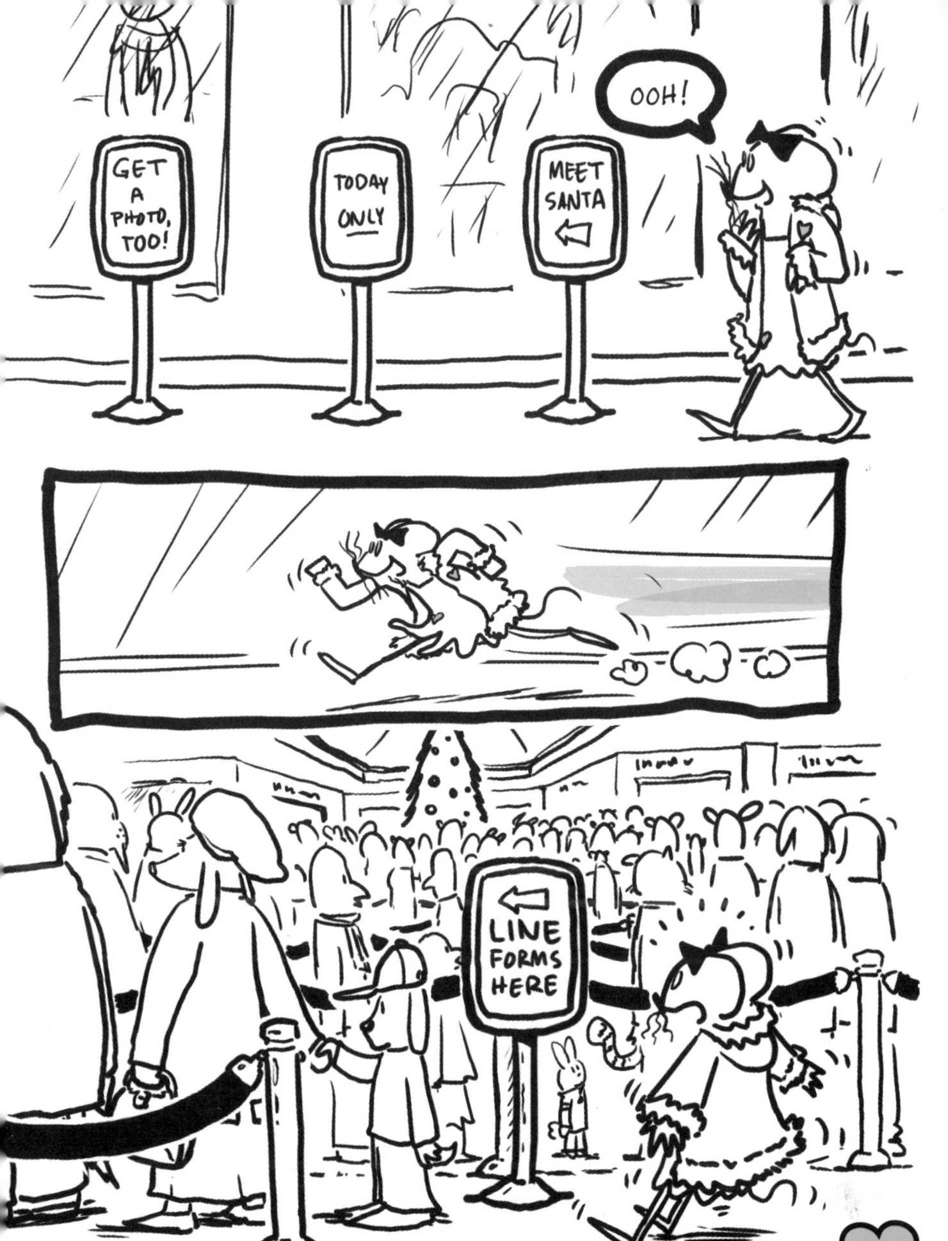
GET A PHOTO, TOO!
TODAY ONLY
MEET SANTA
OOH!
LINE FORMS HERE

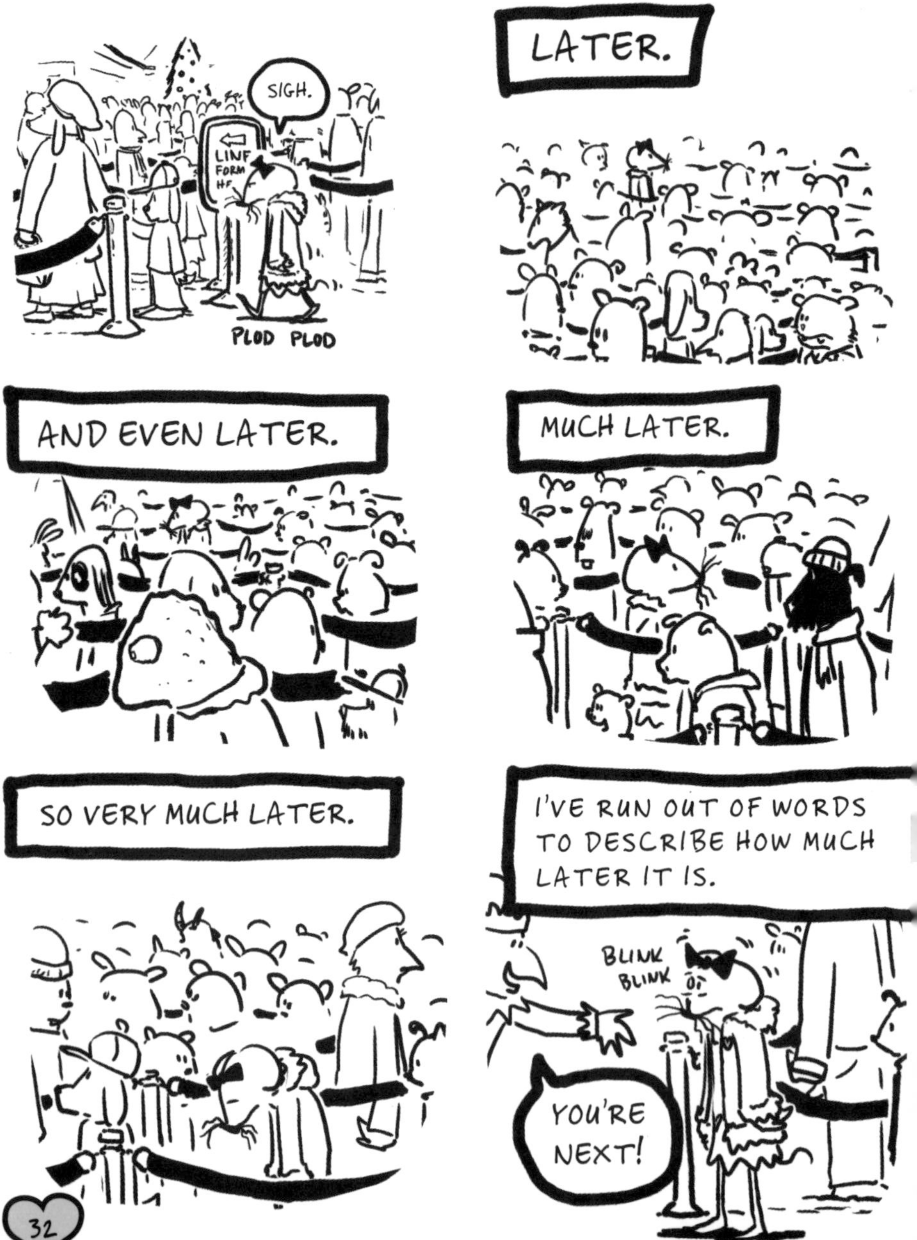
SIGH.
PLOD PLOD
LATER.
AND EVEN LATER.
MUCH LATER.
SO VERY MUCH LATER.
I'VE RUN OUT OF WORDS TO DESCRIBE HOW MUCH LATER IT IS.
BLINK BLINK
YOU'RE NEXT!

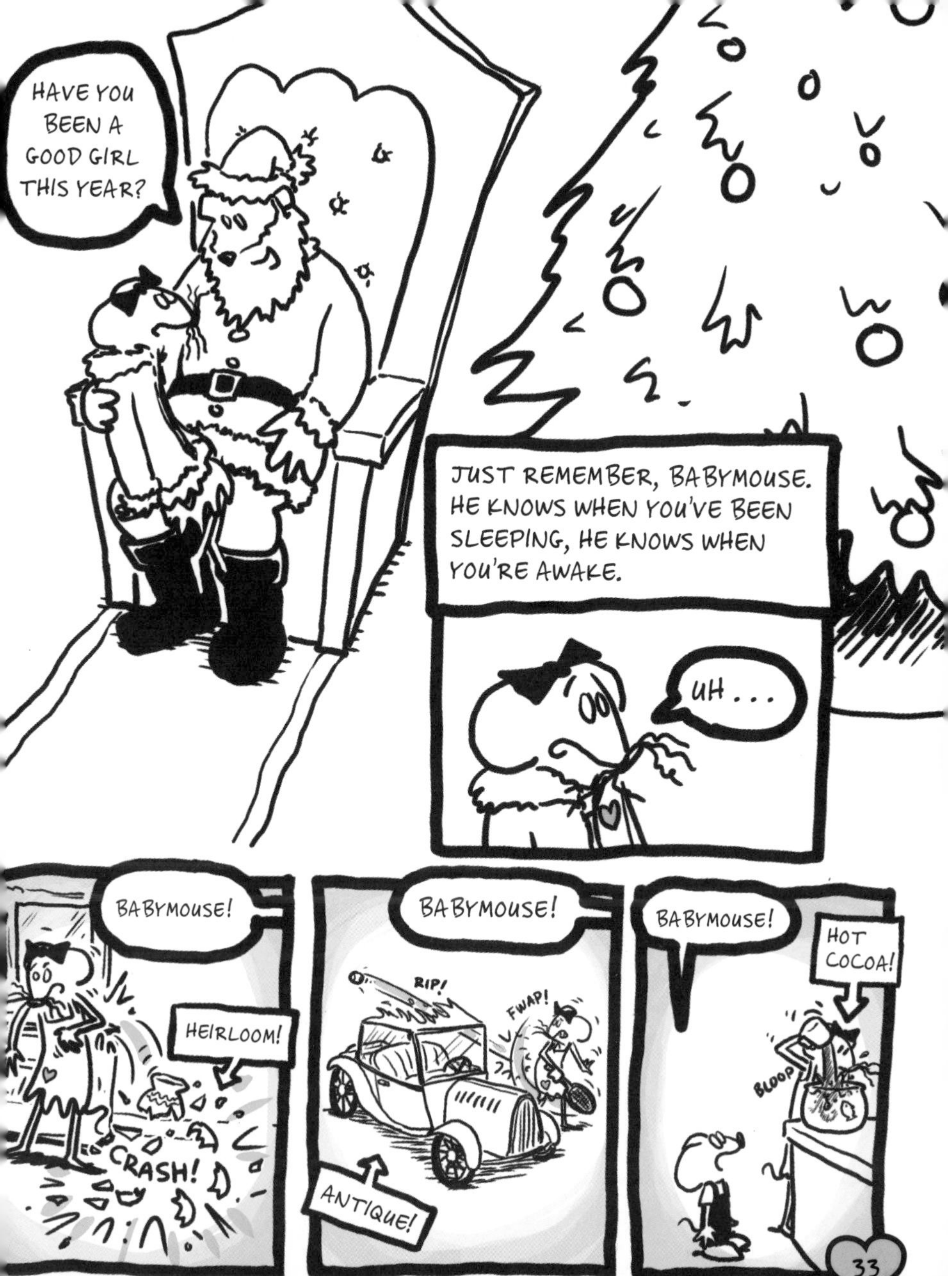
HAVE YOU BEEN A GOOD GIRL THIS YEAR?
JUST REMEMBER, BABYMOUSE. HE KNOWS WHEN YOU'VE BEEN SLEEPING, HE KNOWS WHEN YOU'RE AWAKE.
UH . . .
BABYMOUSE!
HEIRLOOM!
CRASH!
BABYMOUSE!
RIP!
FWAP!
ANTIQUE!
BABYMOUSE!
HOT COCOA!
BLOOP

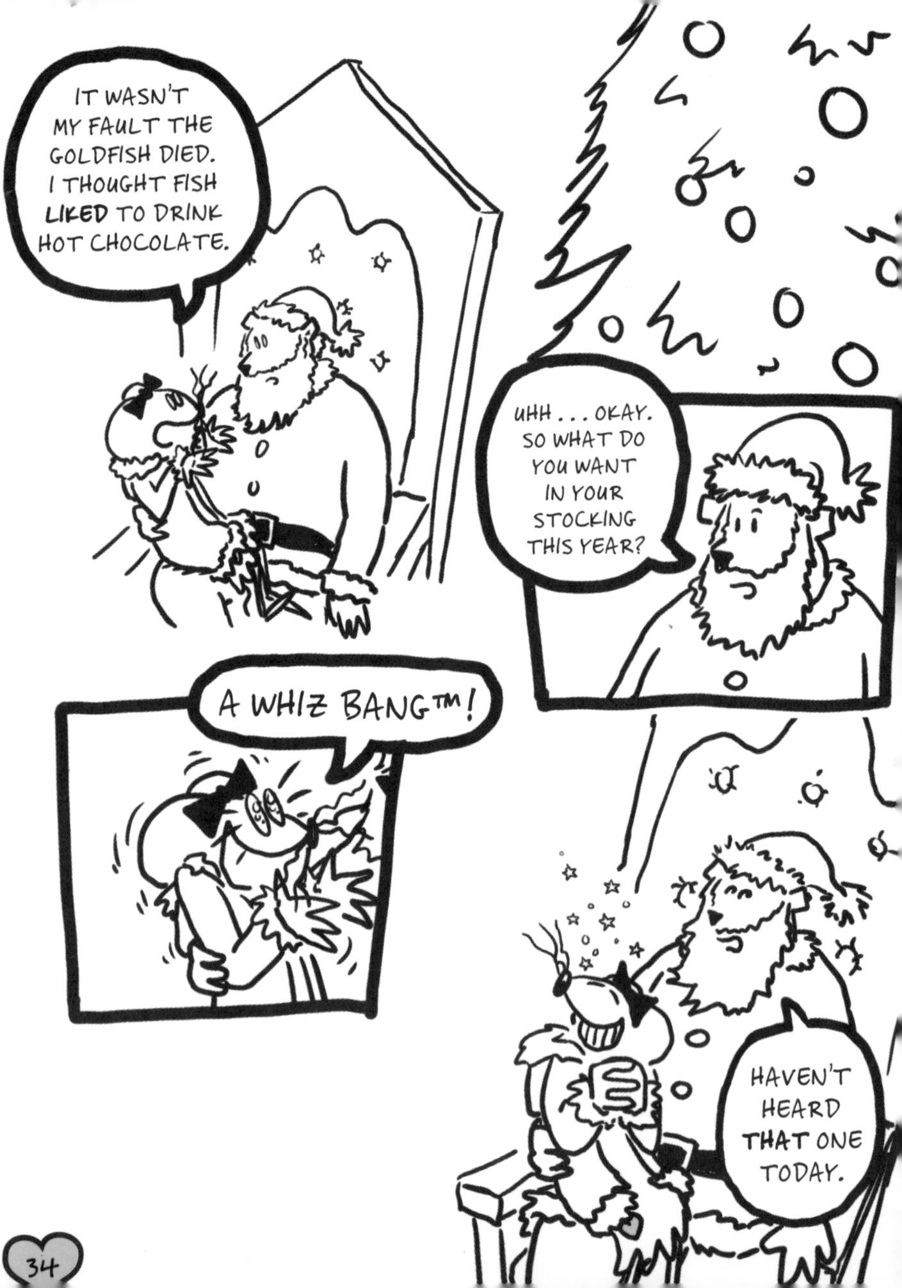
IT WASN'T MY FAULT THE GOLDFISH DIED. I THOUGHT FISH **LIKED** TO DRINK HOT CHOCOLATE.
UHH . . . OKAY. SO WHAT DO YOU WANT IN YOUR STOCKING THIS YEAR?
A WHIZ BANG™!
HAVEN'T HEARD **THAT** ONE TODAY.

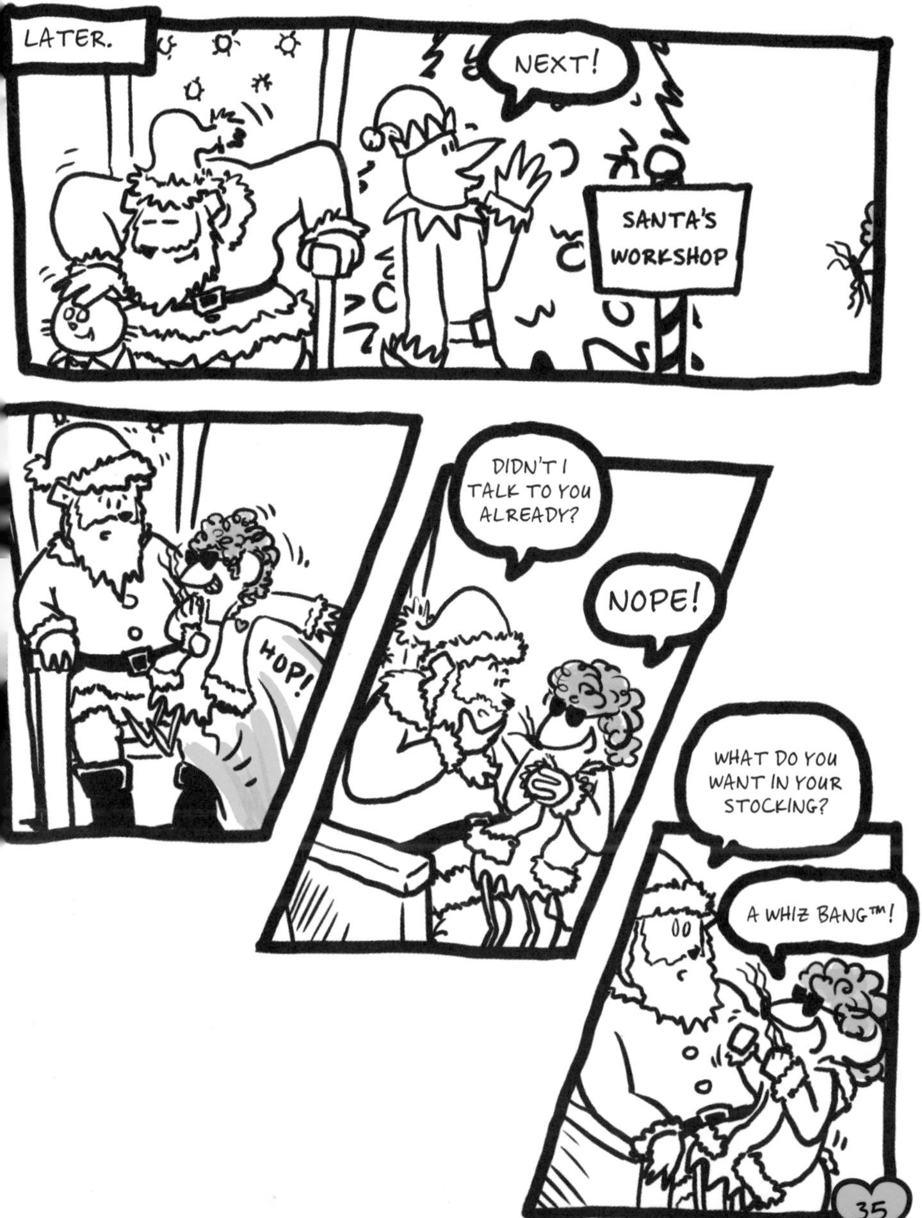
LATER.
NEXT!
SANTA'S WORKSHOP
HOP!
DIDN'T I TALK TO YOU ALREADY?
NOPE!
WHAT DO YOU WANT IN YOUR STOCKING?
A WHIZ BANG™!

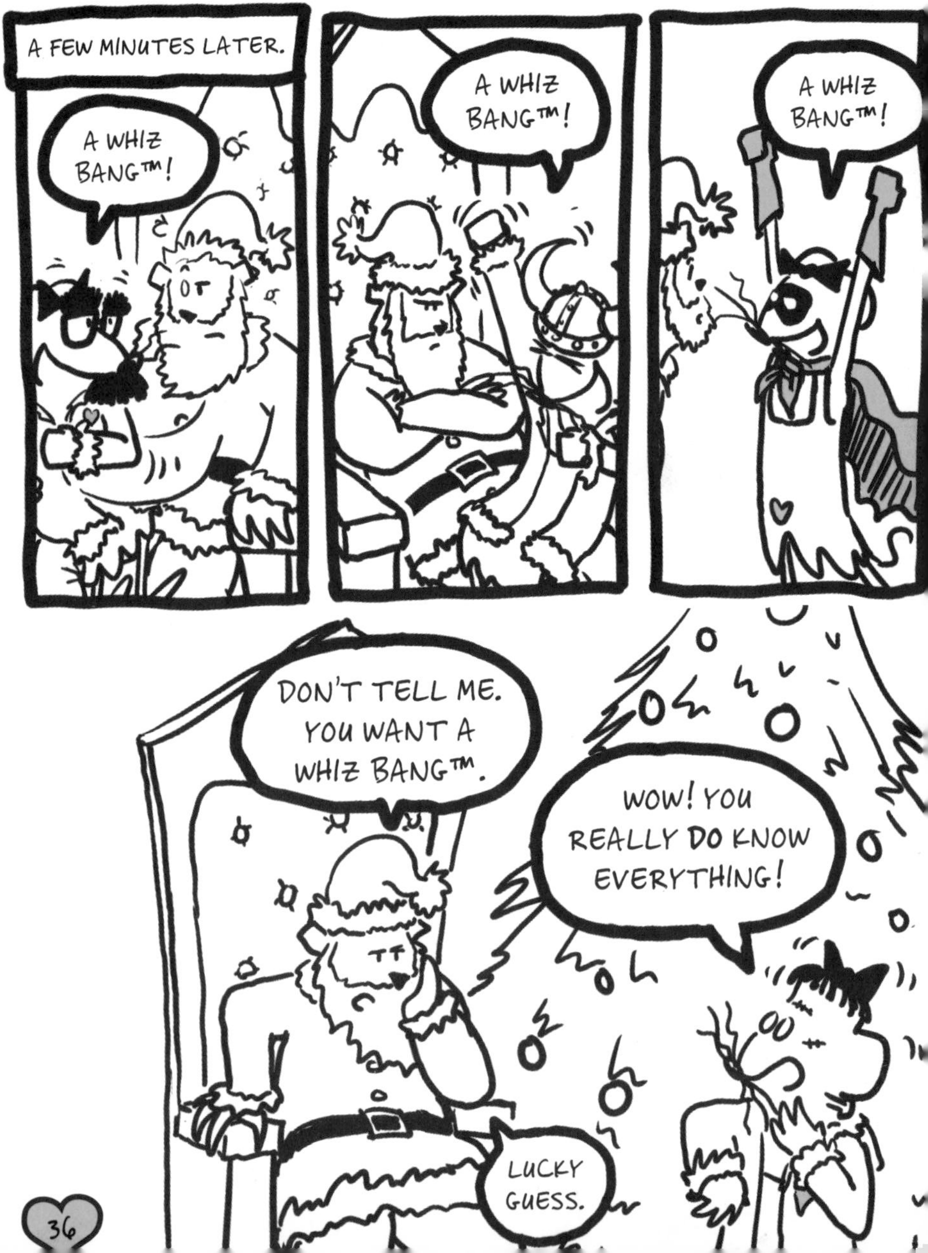
A FEW MINUTES LATER.
A WHIZ BANG™!
A WHIZ BANG™!
A WHIZ BANG™!
DON'T TELL ME. YOU WANT A WHIZ BANG™.
WOW! YOU REALLY DO KNOW EVERYTHING!
LUCKY GUESS.

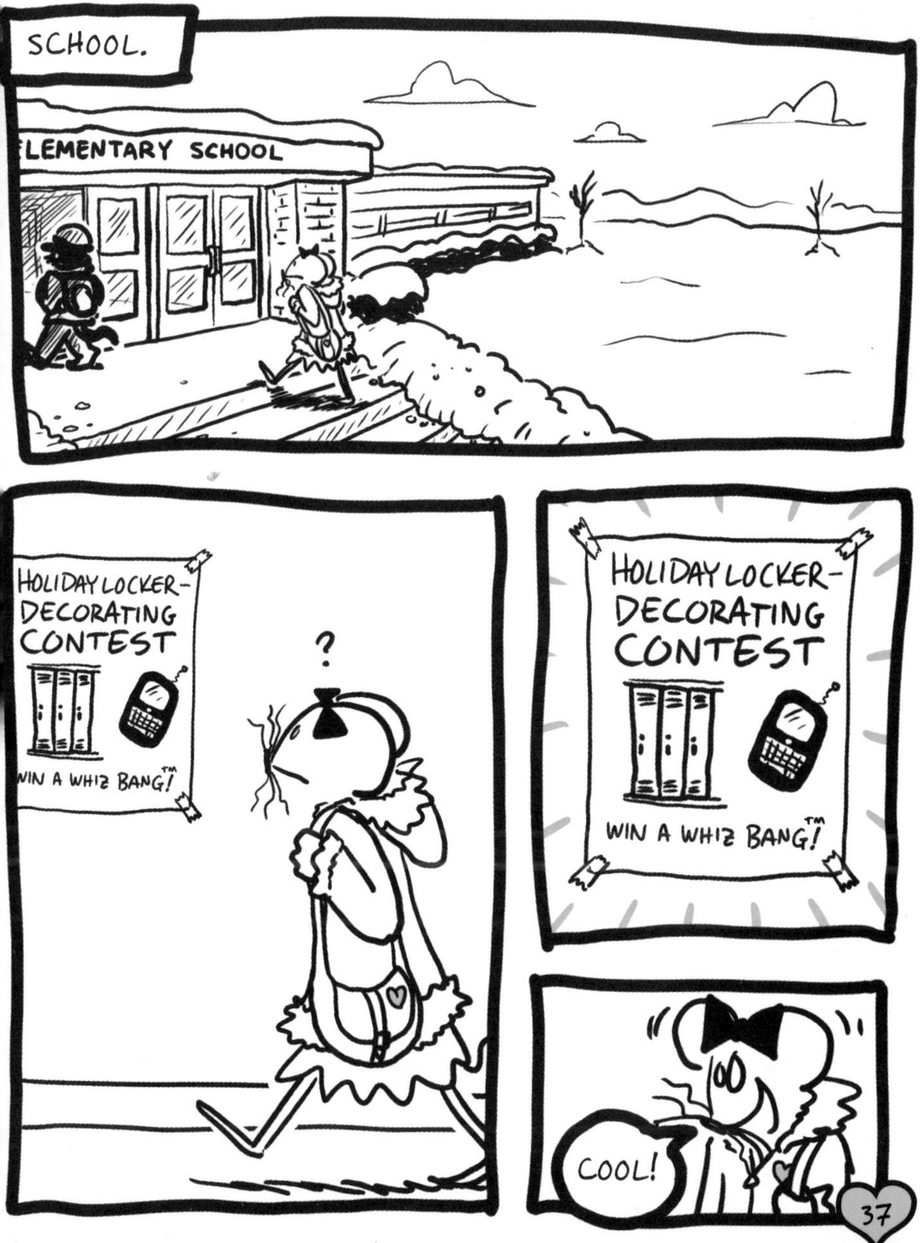
SCHOOL.
ELEMENTARY SCHOOL
HOLIDAY LOCKER-DECORATING CONTEST
WIN A WHIZ BANG!™
?
HOLIDAY LOCKER-DECORATING CONTEST
WIN A WHIZ BANG!™
COOL!

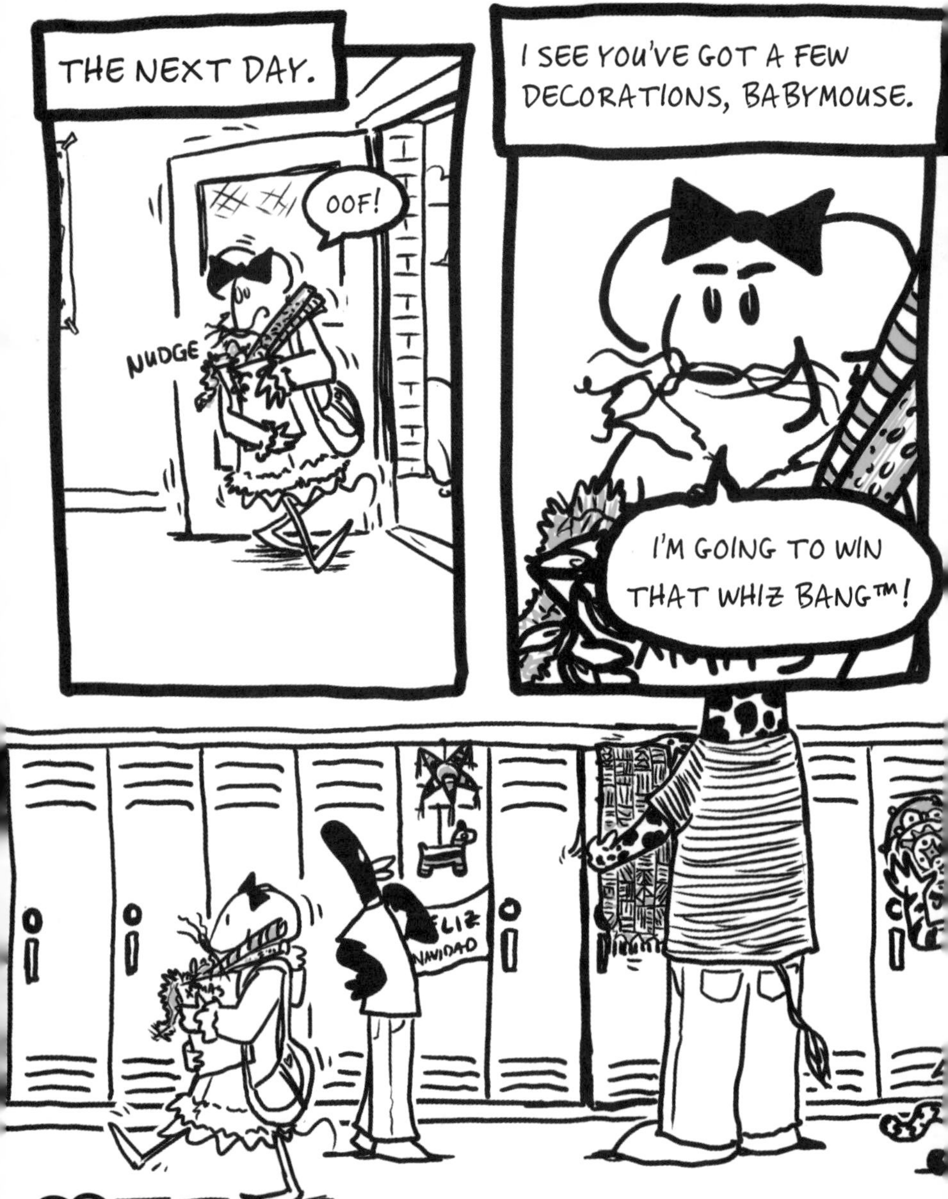
THE NEXT DAY.
OOF!
NUDGE
I SEE YOU'VE GOT A FEW DECORATIONS, BABYMOUSE.
I'M GOING TO WIN THAT WHIZ BANG™!
FELIZ NAVIDAD

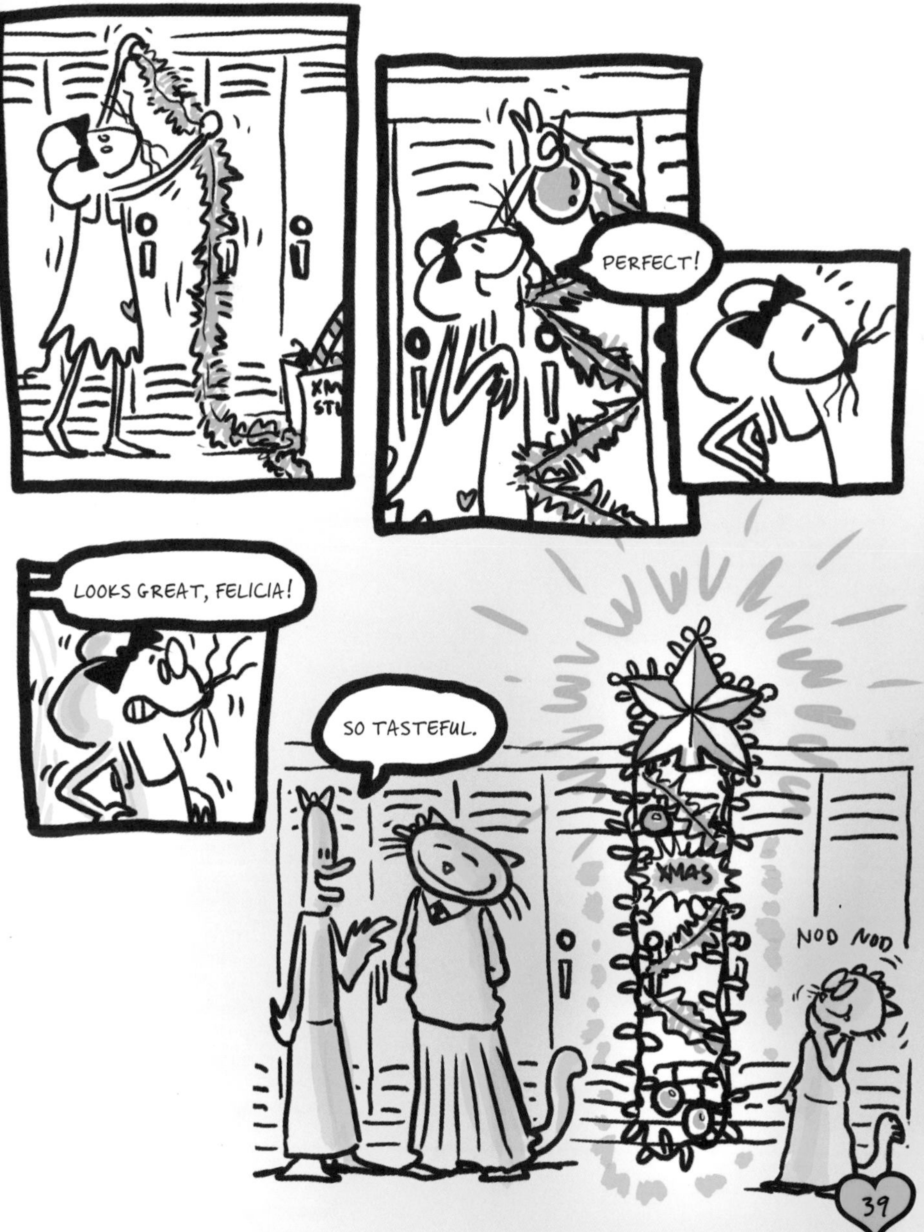
XM
STU
PERFECT!
LOOKS GREAT, FELICIA!
SO TASTEFUL.
XMAS
NOD NOD

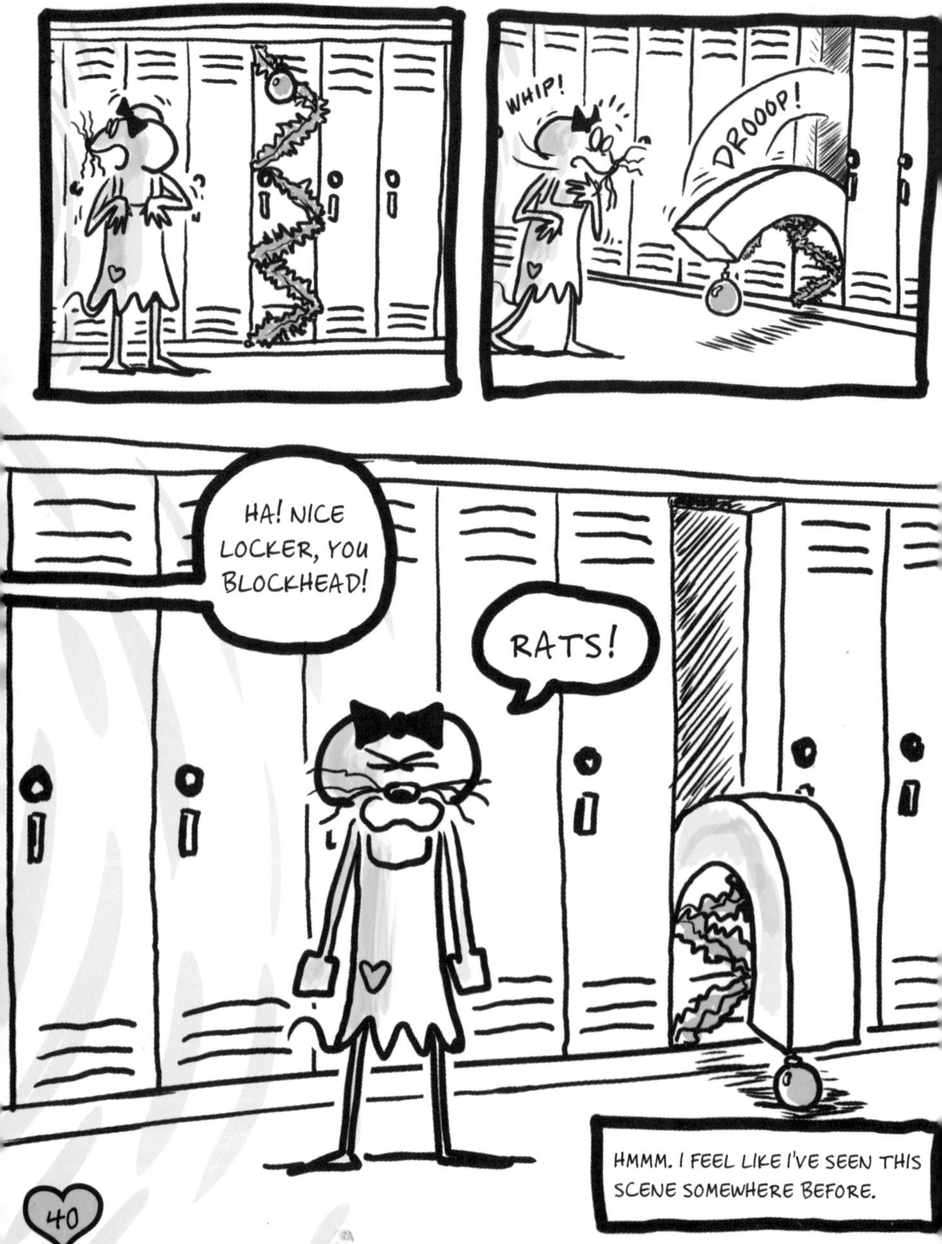
WHIP!
DROOOP!
HA! NICE LOCKER, YOU BLOCKHEAD!
RATS!
HMMM. I FEEL LIKE I'VE SEEN THIS SCENE SOMEWHERE BEFORE.

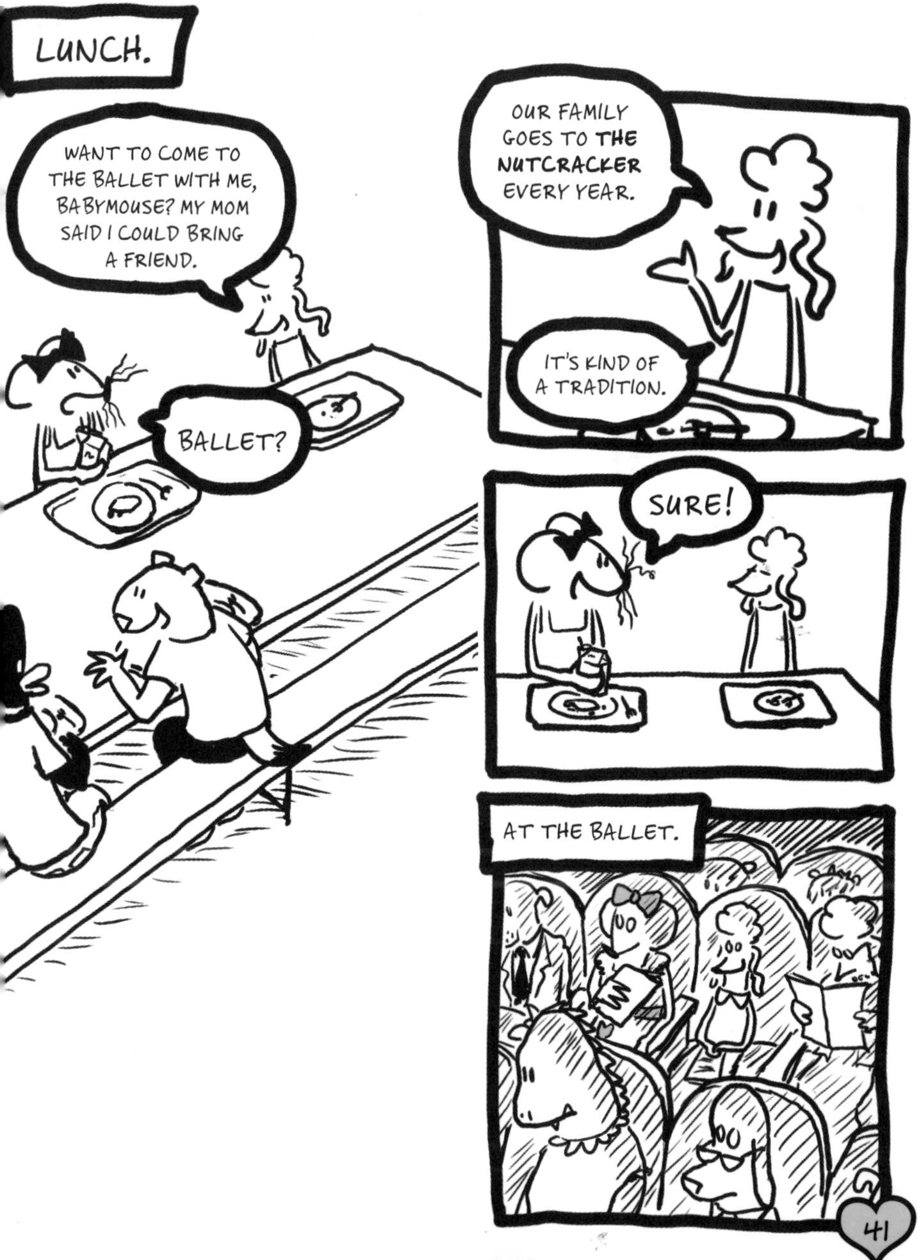
LUNCH.
WANT TO COME TO THE BALLET WITH ME, BABYMOUSE? MY MOM SAID I COULD BRING A FRIEND.
BALLET?
OUR FAMILY GOES TO THE NUTCRACKER EVERY YEAR.
IT'S KIND OF A TRADITION.
SURE!
AT THE BALLET.

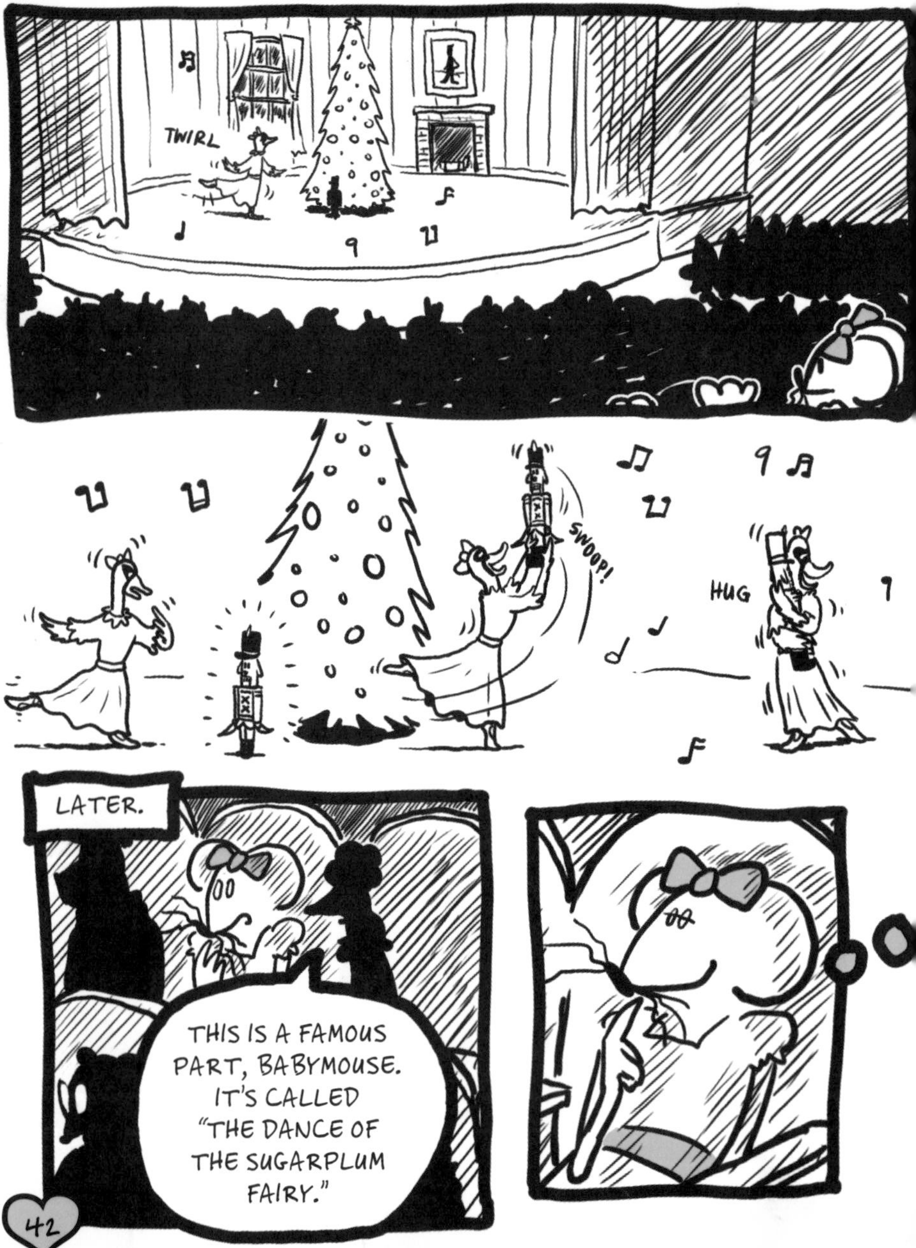
TWIRL
SWOOP!
HUG
LATER.
THIS IS A FAMOUS PART, BABYMOUSE. IT'S CALLED "THE DANCE OF THE SUGARPLUM FAIRY."

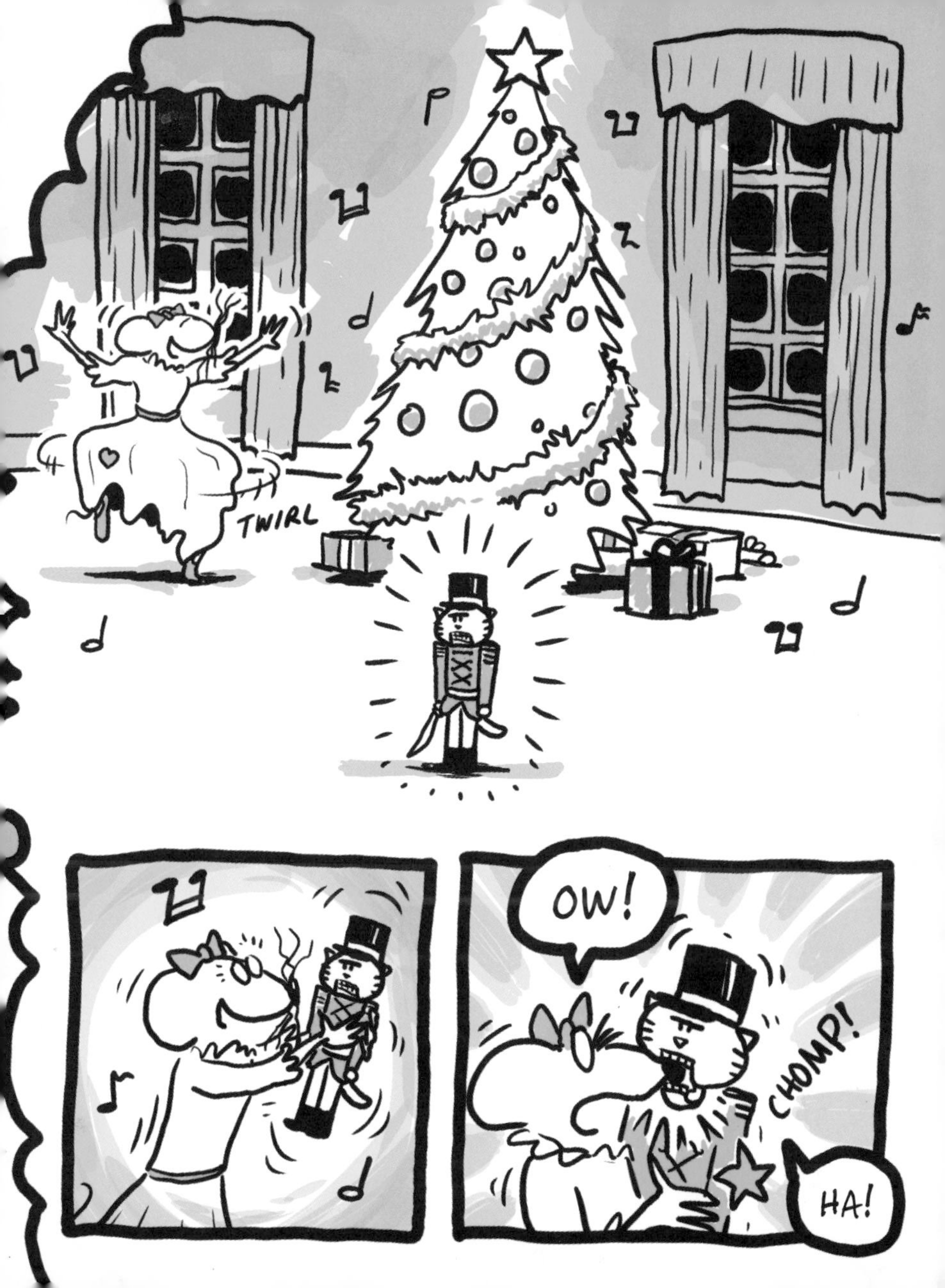
TWIRL
OW!
CHOMP!
HA!

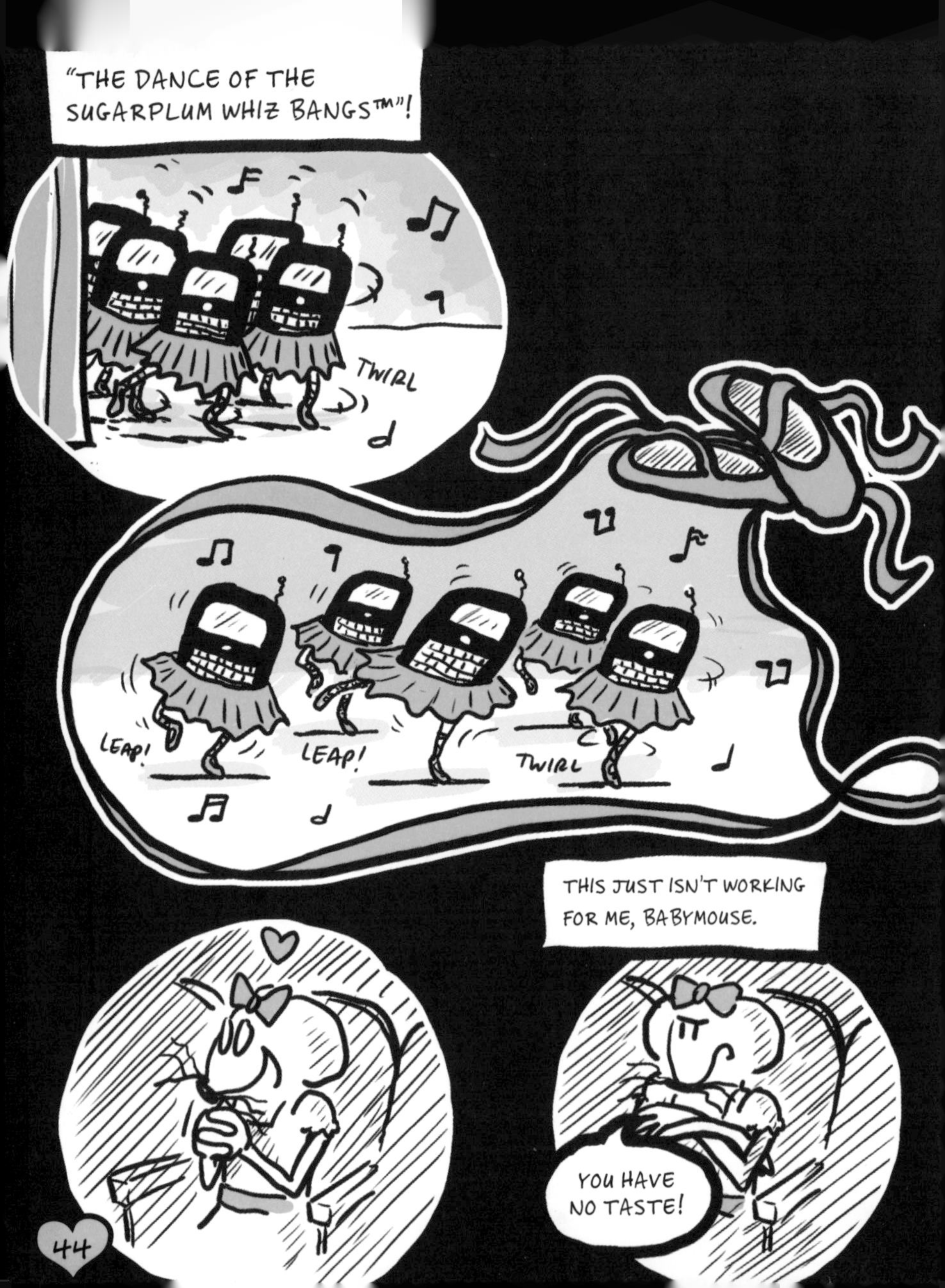

"THE DANCE OF THE SUGARPLUM WHIZ BANGS™"!
TWIRL
LEAP!
LEAP!
TWIRL
THIS JUST ISN'T WORKING FOR ME, BABYMOUSE.
YOU HAVE NO TASTE!

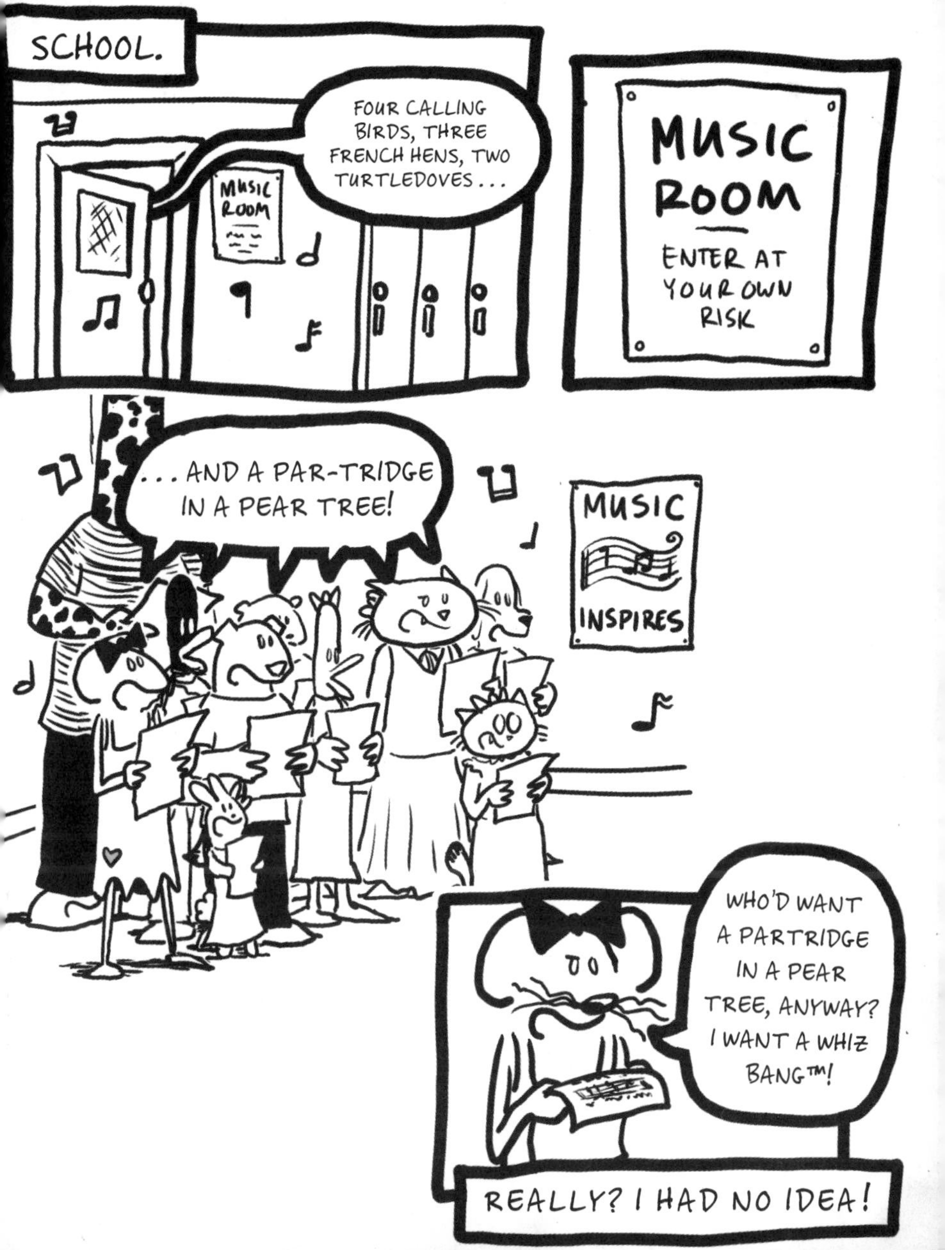
SCHOOL.
FOUR CALLING BIRDS, THREE FRENCH HENS, TWO TURTLEDOVES . . .
MUSIC ROOM
MUSIC ROOM
ENTER AT YOUR OWN RISK
. . . AND A PAR-TRIDGE IN A PEAR TREE!
MUSIC
INSPIRES
WHO'D WANT A PARTRIDGE IN A PEAR TREE, ANYWAY? I WANT A WHIZ BANG™!
REALLY? I HAD NO IDEA!

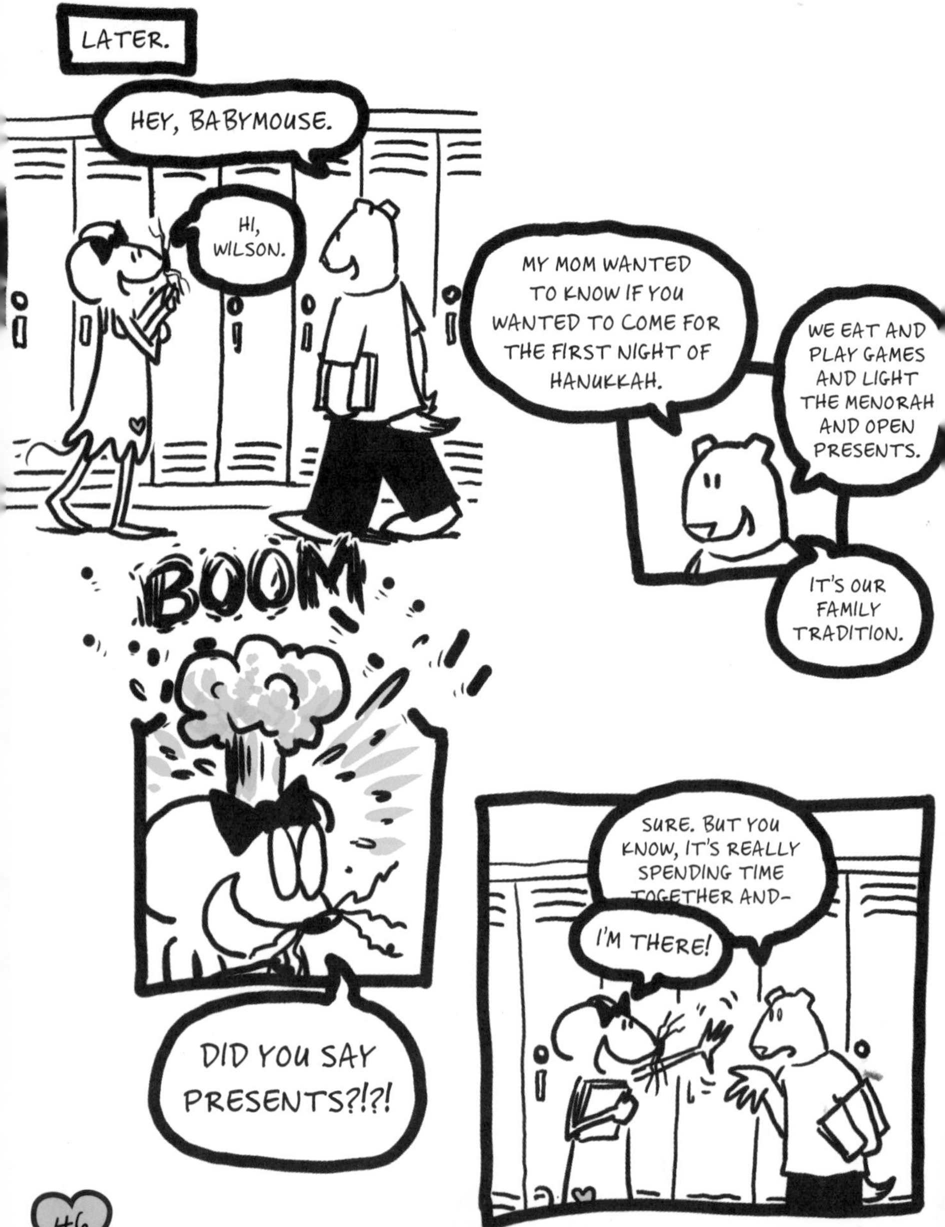
LATER.
HEY, BABYMOUSE.
HI, WILSON.
MY MOM WANTED TO KNOW IF YOU WANTED TO COME FOR THE FIRST NIGHT OF HANUKKAH.
WE EAT AND PLAY GAMES AND LIGHT THE MENORAH AND OPEN PRESENTS.
IT'S OUR FAMILY TRADITION.
BOOM
DID YOU SAY PRESENTS?!?!
SURE. BUT YOU KNOW, IT'S REALLY SPENDING TIME TOGETHER AND–
I'M THERE!

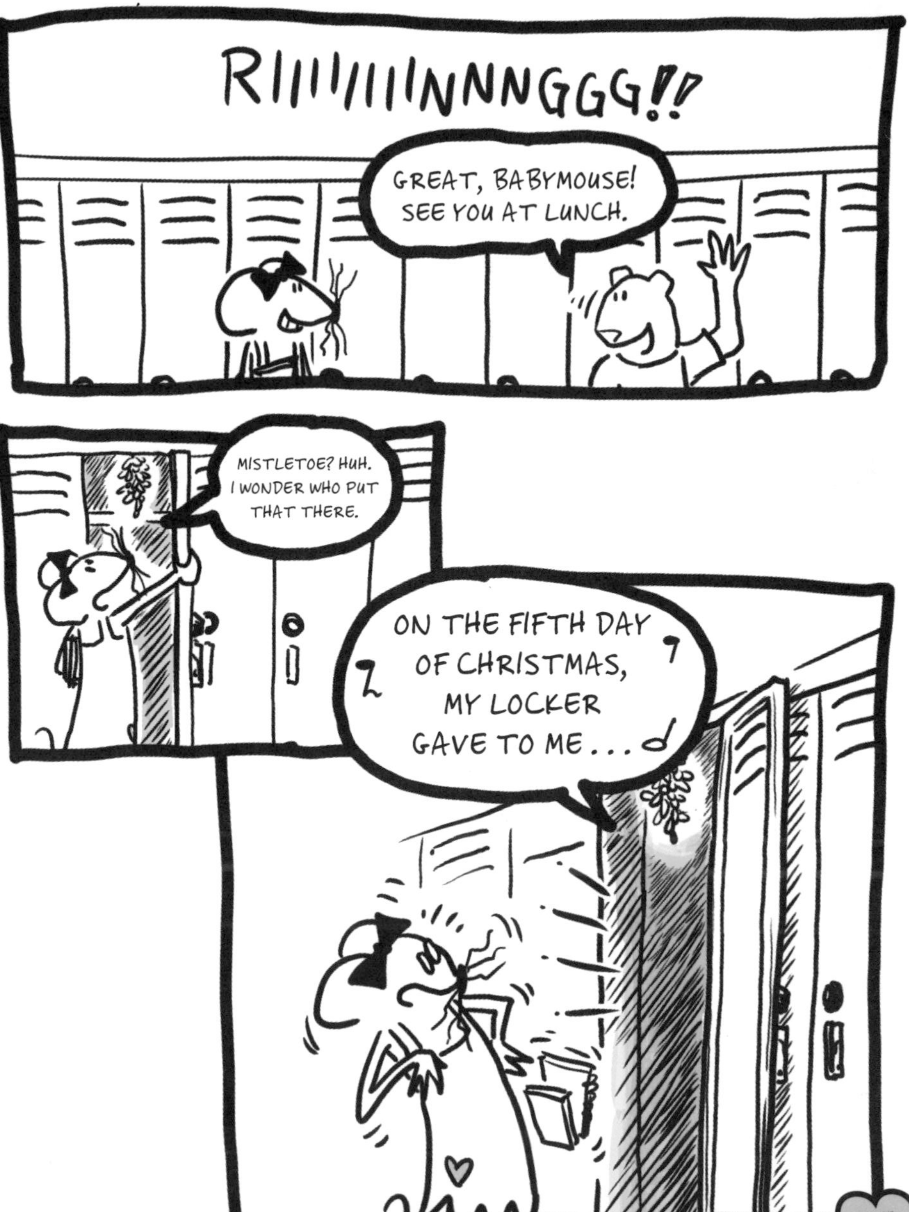
RIIIIIIIINNNGGG!!
GREAT, BABYMOUSE! SEE YOU AT LUNCH.
MISTLETOE? HUH. I WONDER WHO PUT THAT THERE.
ON THE FIFTH DAY OF CHRISTMAS, MY LOCKER GAVE TO ME...

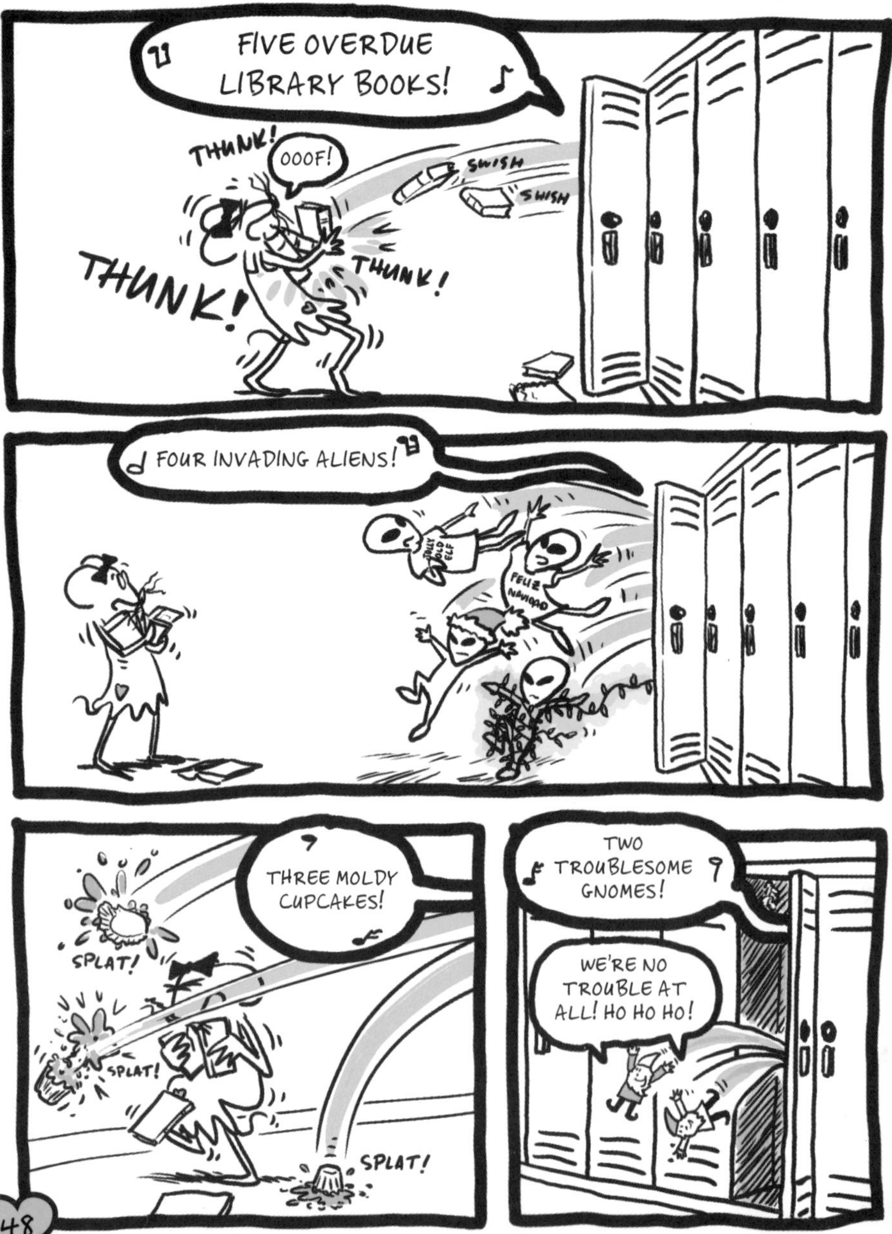
FIVE OVERDUE LIBRARY BOOKS!
THUNK!
OOOF!
SWISH
SWISH
THUNK!
THUNK!
FOUR INVADING ALIENS!
JOLLY OLD ELF
FELIZ NAVIDAD
THREE MOLDY CUPCAKES!
SPLAT!
SPLAT!
SPLAT!
TWO TROUBLESOME GNOMES!
WE'RE NO TROUBLE AT ALL! HO HO HO!

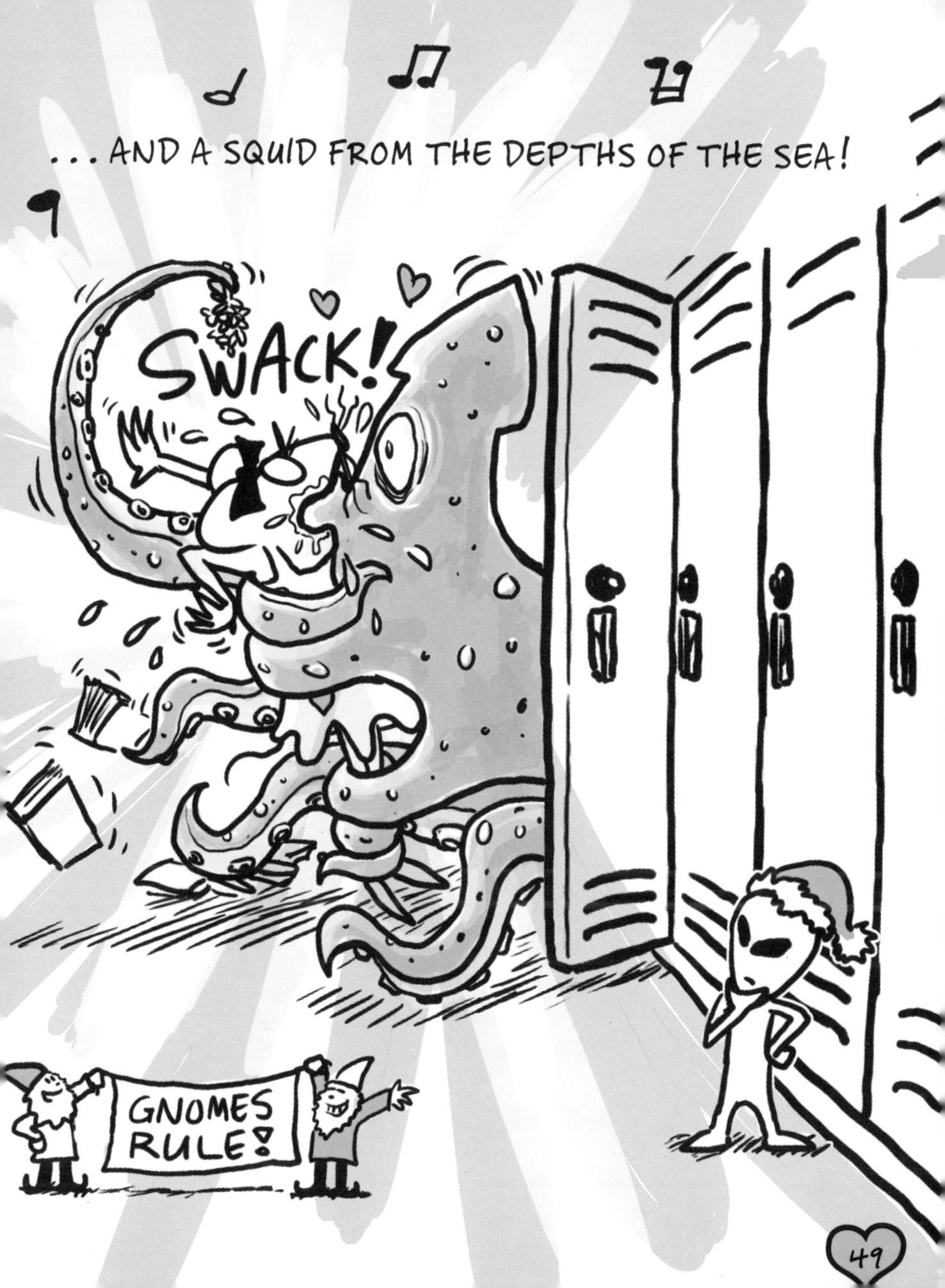

...AND A SQUID FROM THE DEPTHS OF THE SEA!
SWACK!
GNOMES RULE!

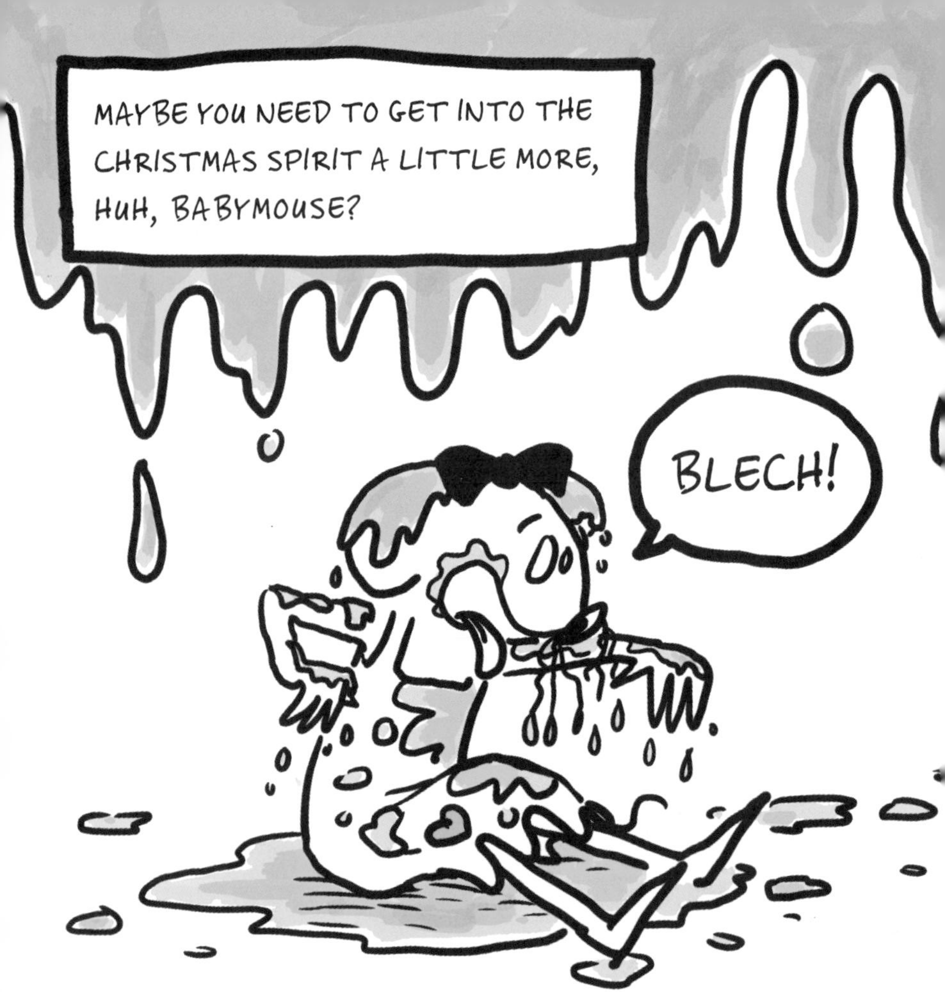
MAYBE YOU NEED TO GET INTO THE CHRISTMAS SPIRIT A LITTLE MORE, HUH, BABYMOUSE?
BLECH!

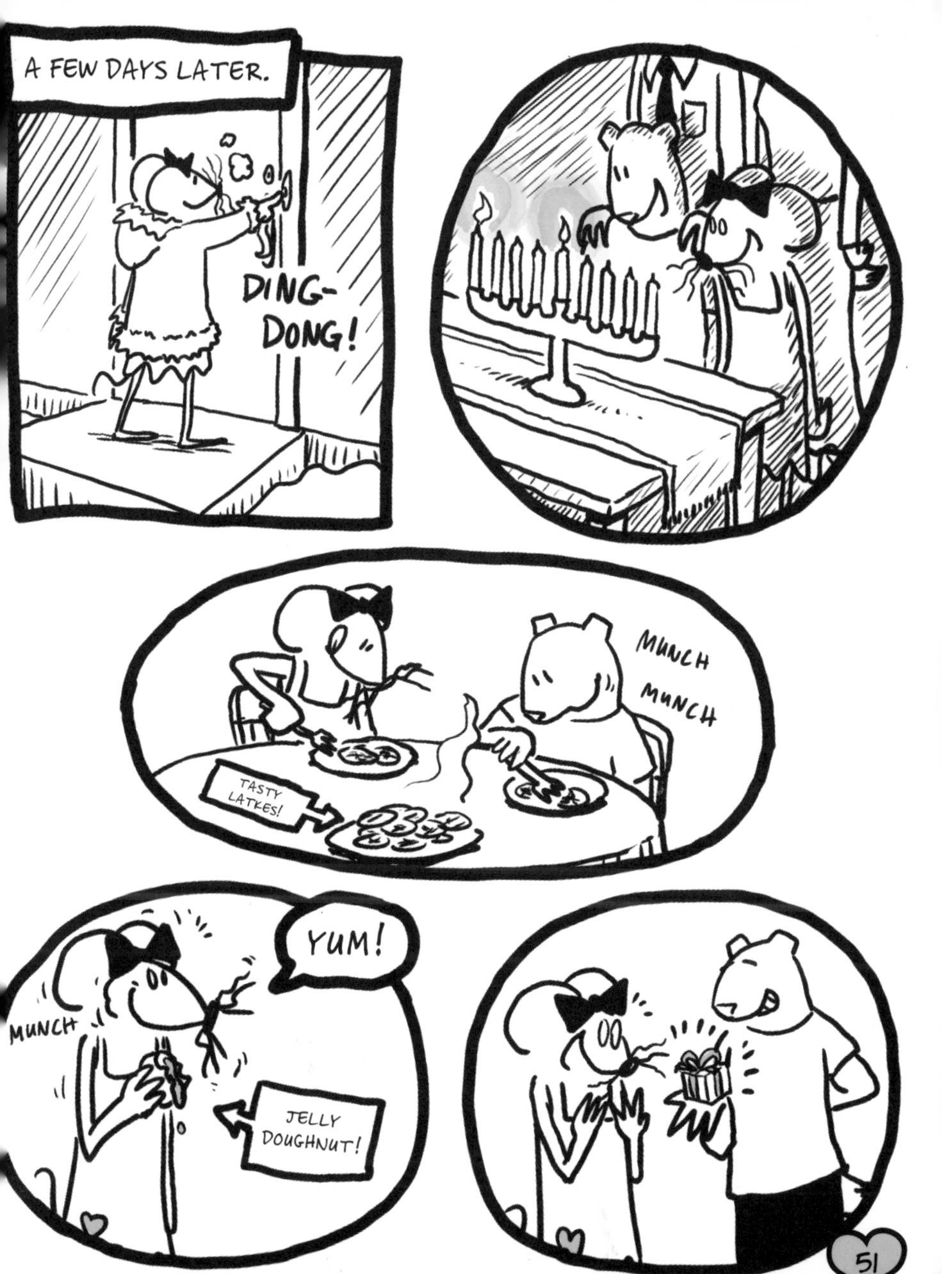
A FEW DAYS LATER.
DING-DONG!
MUNCH MUNCH
TASTY LATKES!
YUM!
MUNCH
JELLY DOUGHNUT!

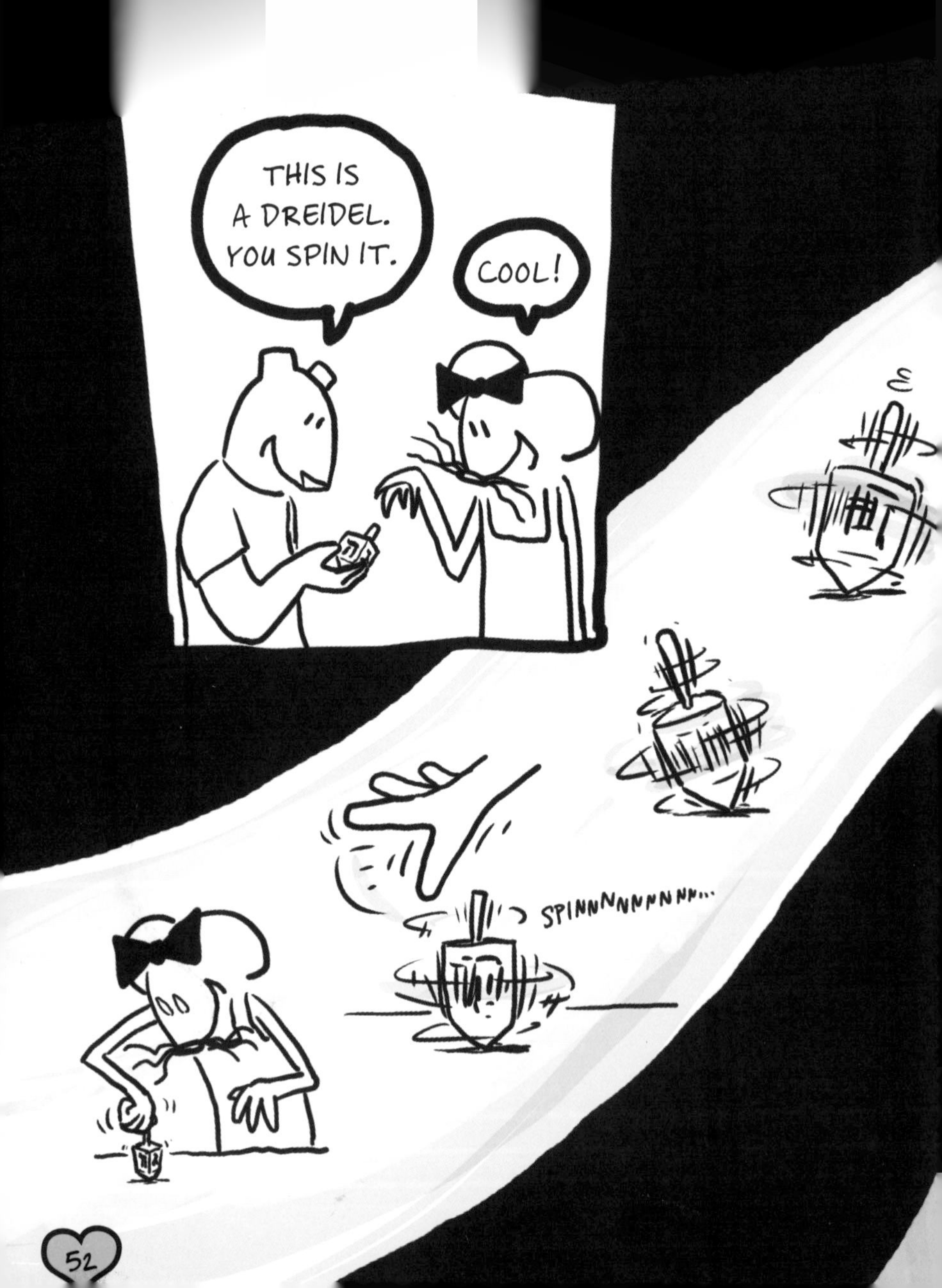
THIS IS A DREIDEL. YOU SPIN IT.
COOL!
SPINNNNNNNNN...

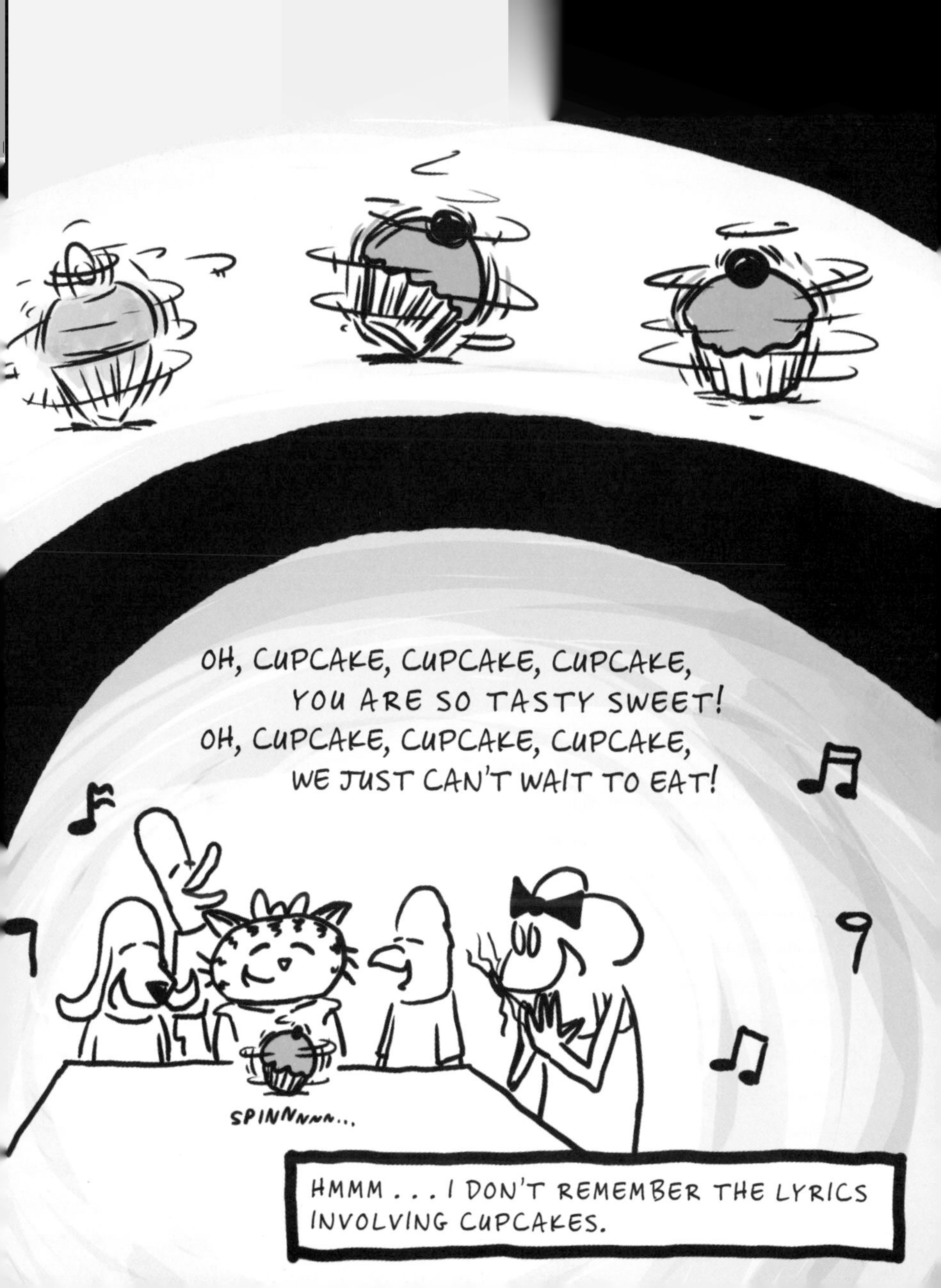

OH, CUPCAKE, CUPCAKE, CUPCAKE,
YOU ARE SO TASTY SWEET!
OH, CUPCAKE, CUPCAKE, CUPCAKE,
WE JUST CAN'T WAIT TO EAT!
SPINNNNN...
HMMM . . . I DON'T REMEMBER THE LYRICS INVOLVING CUPCAKES.

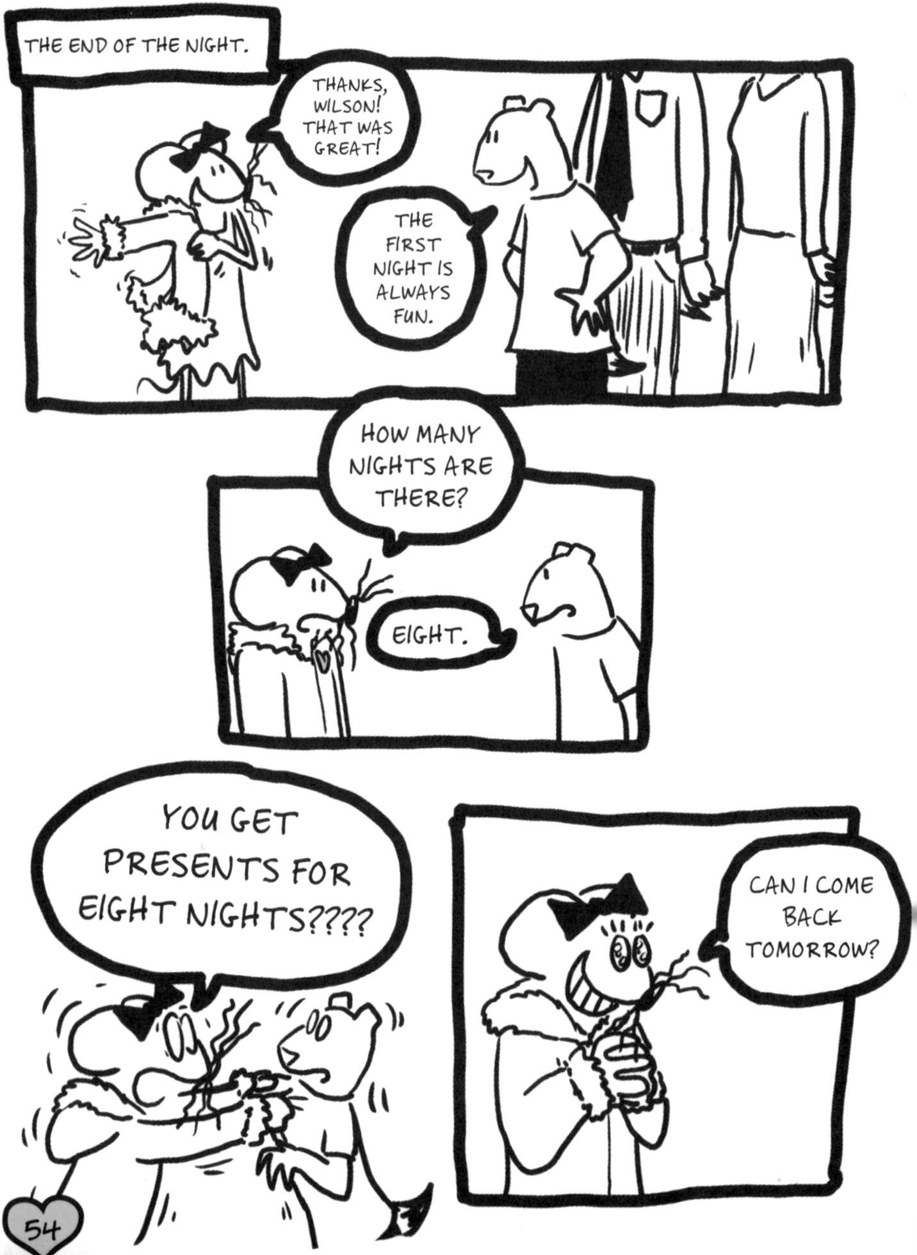
THE END OF THE NIGHT.
THANKS, WILSON! THAT WAS GREAT!
THE FIRST NIGHT IS ALWAYS FUN.
HOW MANY NIGHTS ARE THERE?
EIGHT.
YOU GET PRESENTS FOR EIGHT NIGHTS????
CAN I COME BACK TOMORROW?

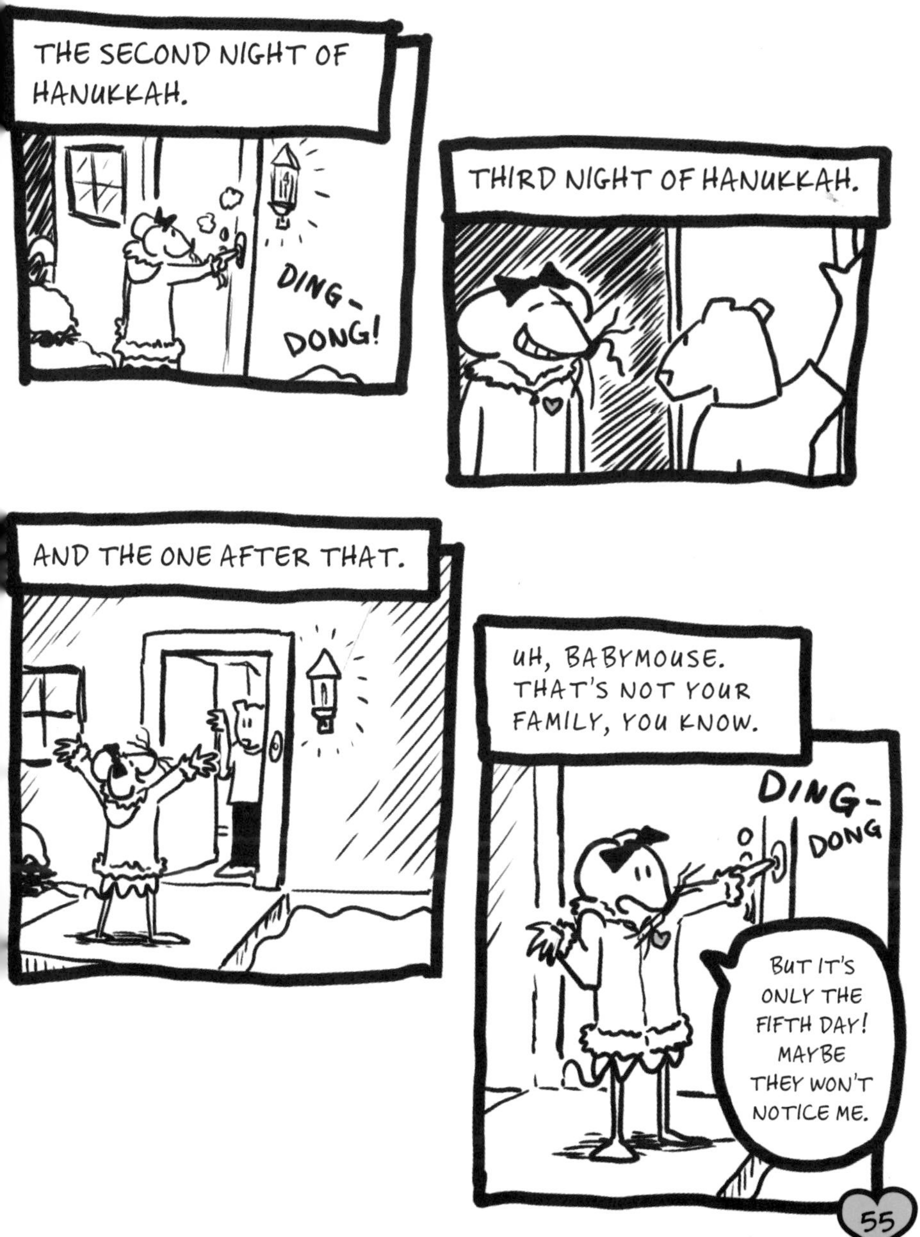
THE SECOND NIGHT OF HANUKKAH.
DING-DONG!
THIRD NIGHT OF HANUKKAH.
AND THE ONE AFTER THAT.
UH, BABYMOUSE. THAT'S NOT YOUR FAMILY, YOU KNOW.
DING-DONG
BUT IT'S ONLY THE FIFTH DAY! MAYBE THEY WON'T NOTICE ME.

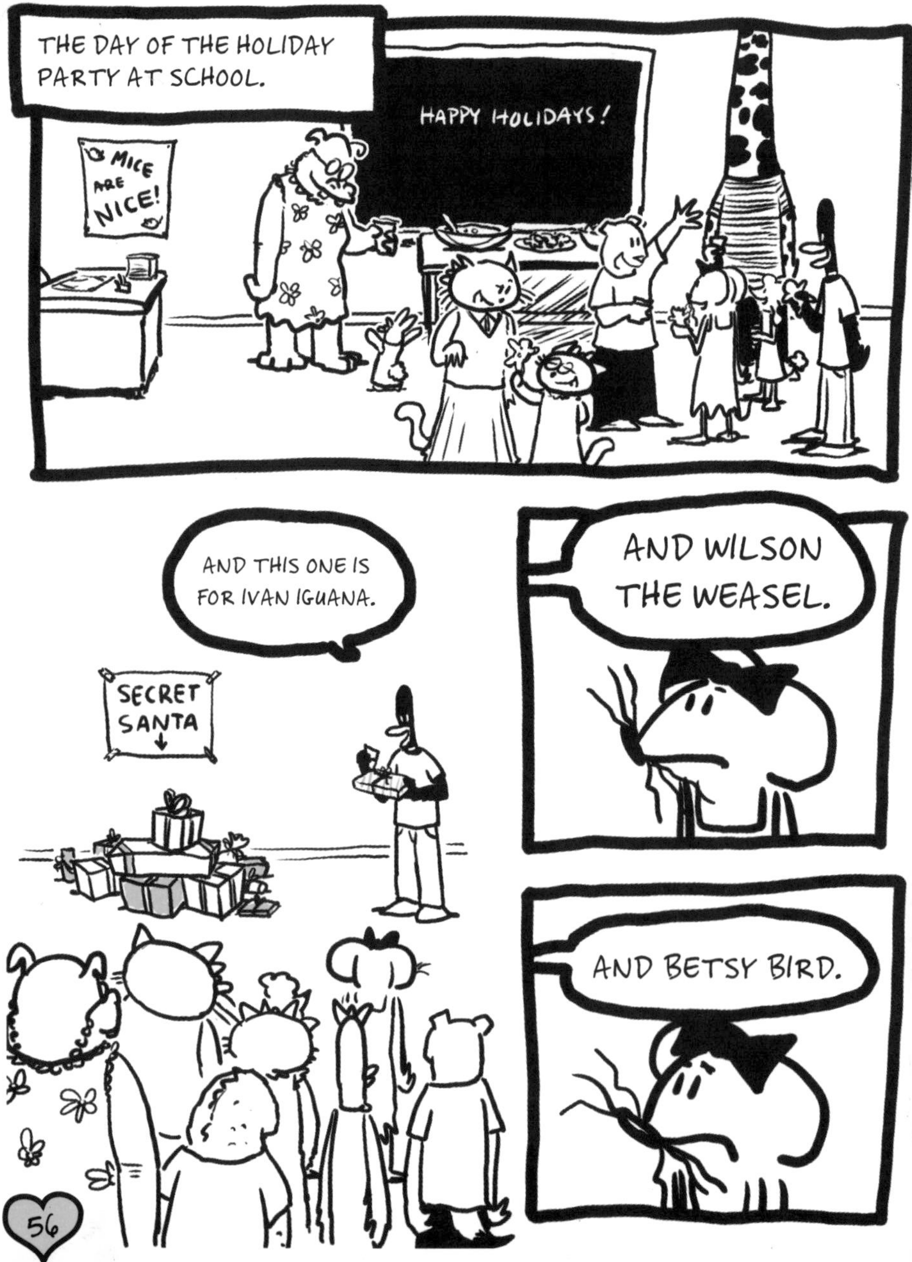
THE DAY OF THE HOLIDAY PARTY AT SCHOOL.
HAPPY HOLIDAYS!
MICE ARE NICE!
AND THIS ONE IS FOR IVAN IGUANA.
SECRET SANTA
AND WILSON THE WEASEL.
AND BETSY BIRD.

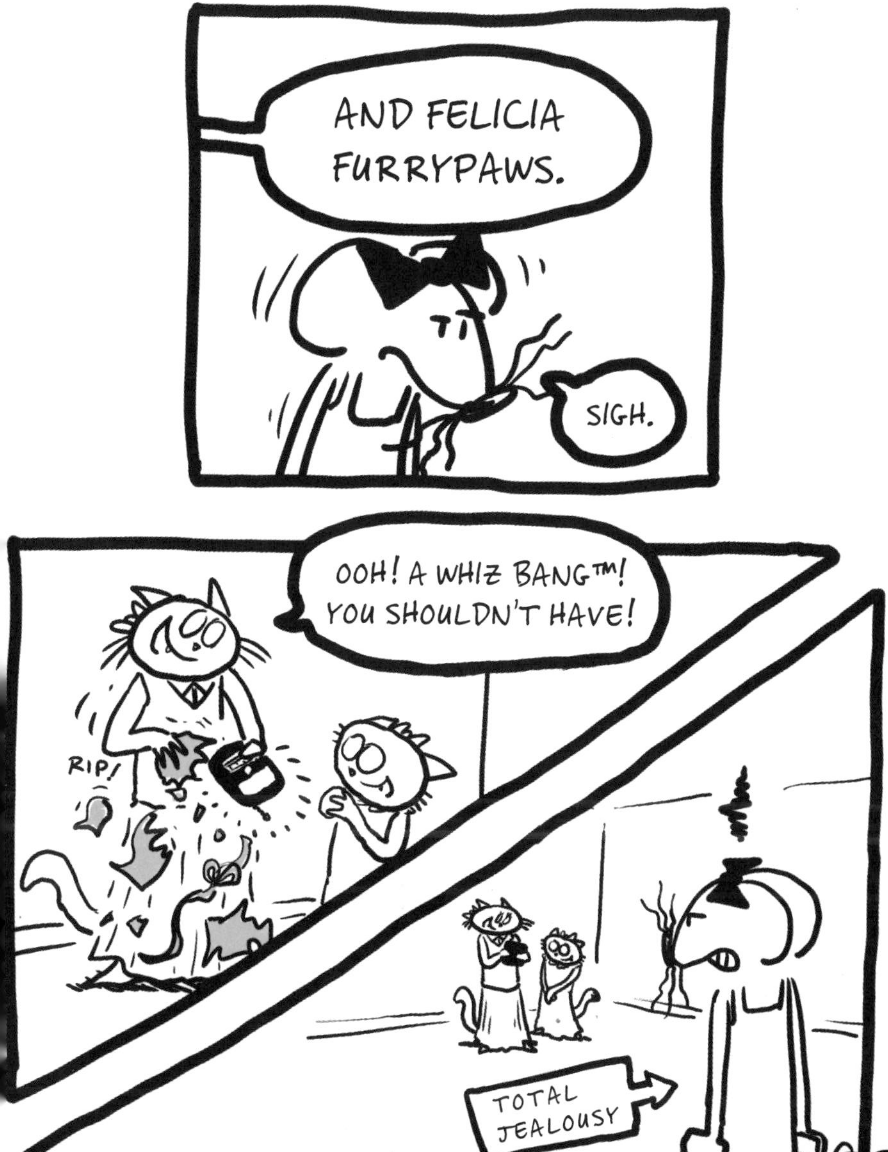
AND FELICIA FURRYPAWS.
SIGH.
OOH! A WHIZ BANG™! YOU SHOULDN'T HAVE!
RIP!
TOTAL JEALOUSY

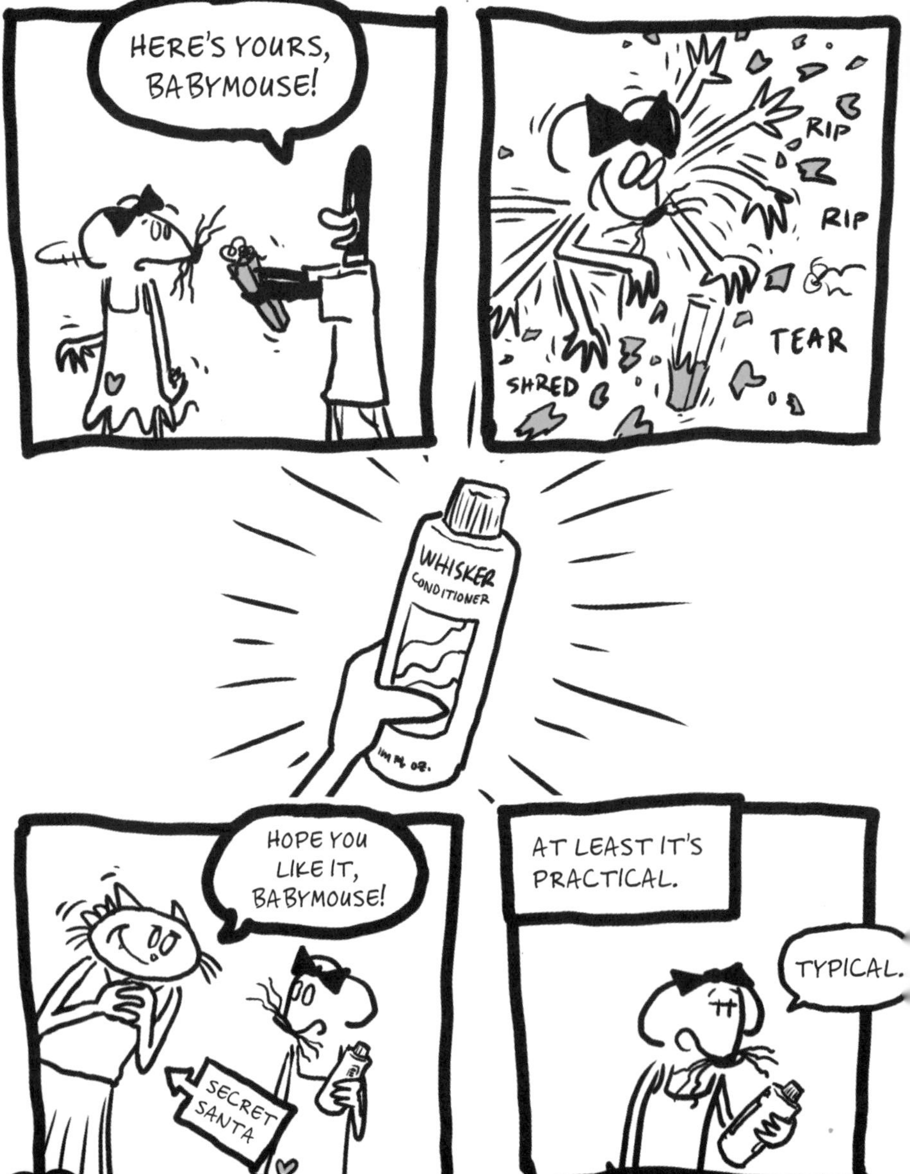
HERE'S YOURS, BABYMOUSE!
RIP
RIP
TEAR
SHRED
WHISKER CONDITIONER
HOPE YOU LIKE IT, BABYMOUSE!
SECRET SANTA
AT LEAST IT'S PRACTICAL.
TYPICAL.

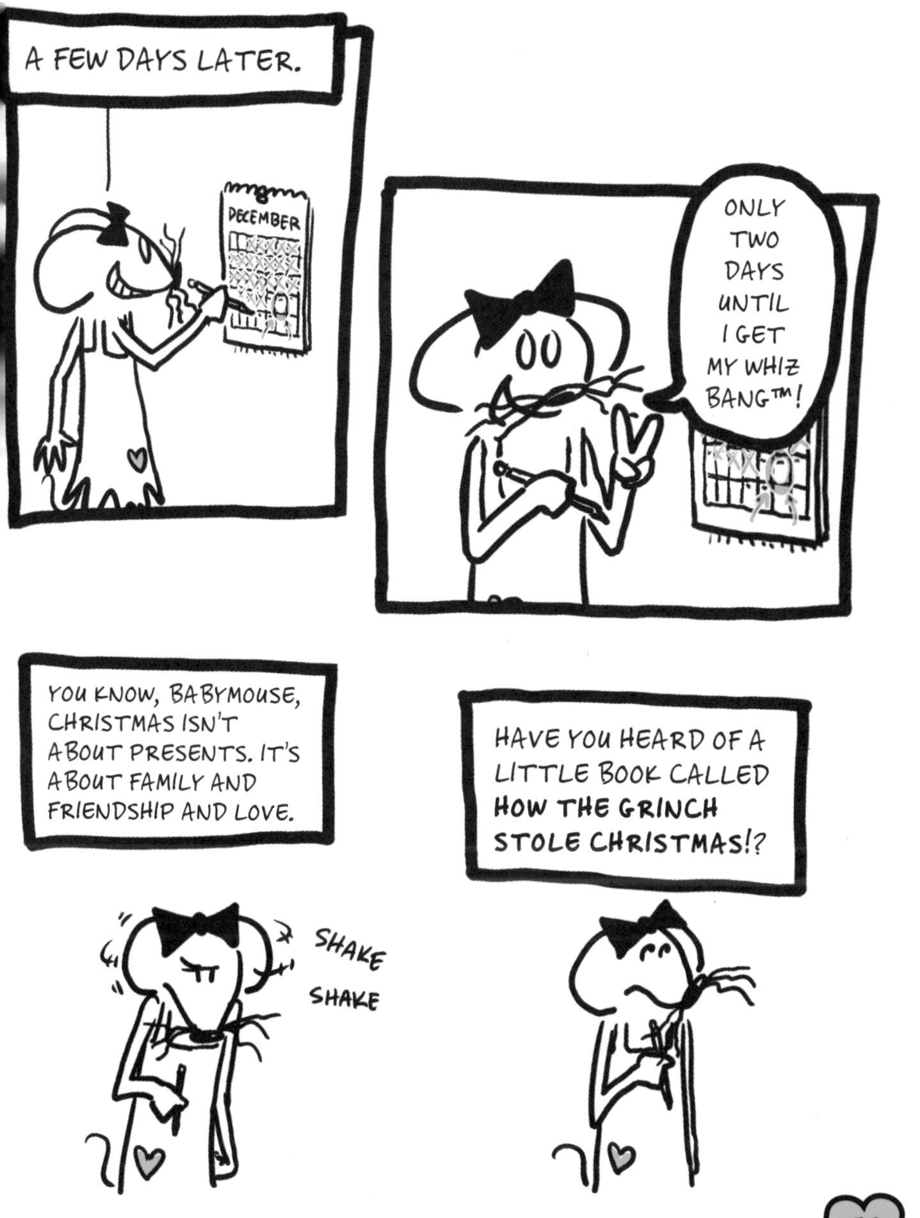
A FEW DAYS LATER.
DECEMBER
ONLY TWO DAYS UNTIL I GET MY WHIZ BANG™!
YOU KNOW, BABYMOUSE, CHRISTMAS ISN'T ABOUT PRESENTS. IT'S ABOUT FAMILY AND FRIENDSHIP AND LOVE.
SHAKE
SHAKE
HAVE YOU HEARD OF A LITTLE BOOK CALLED **HOW THE GRINCH STOLE CHRISTMAS**!?

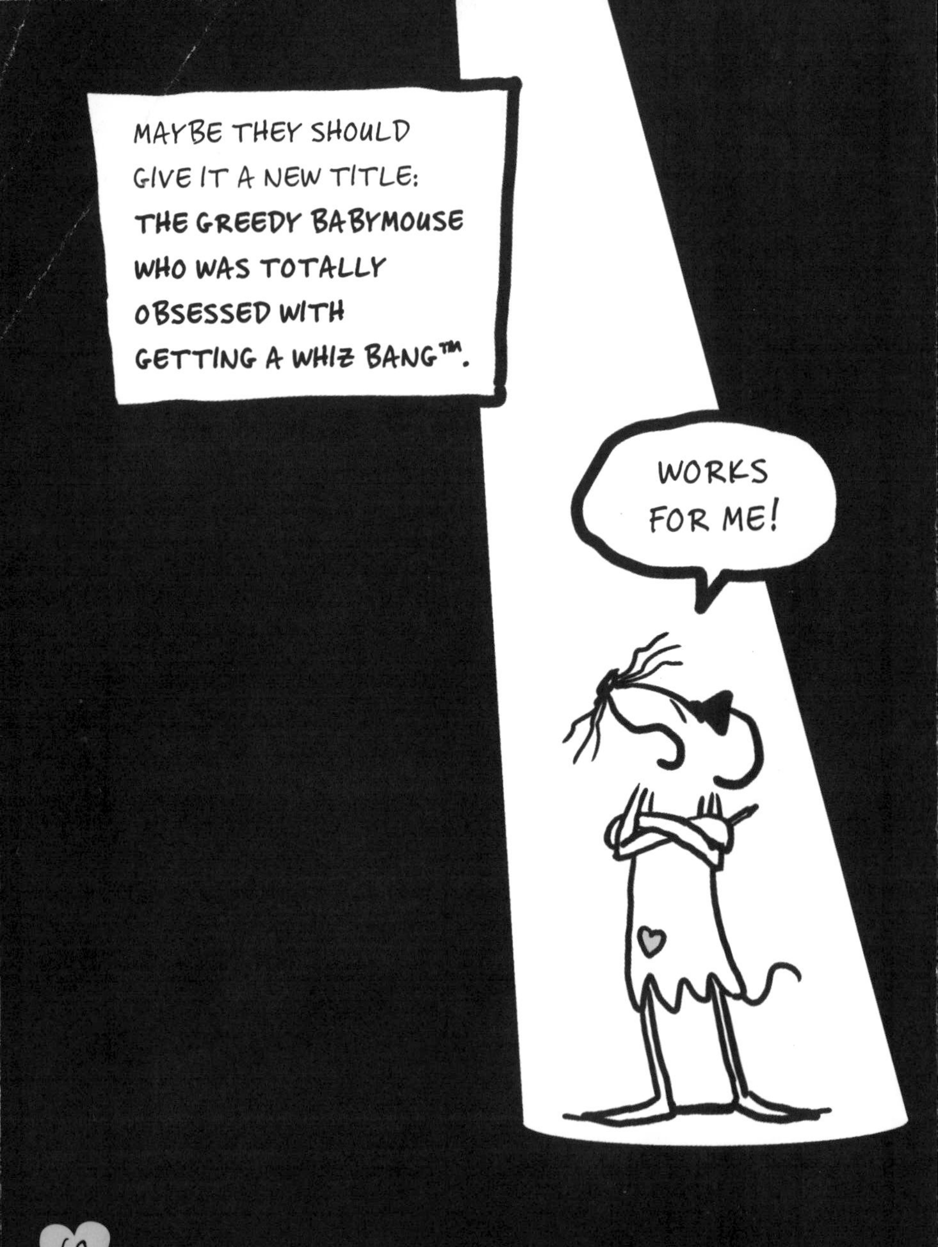
MAYBE THEY SHOULD GIVE IT A NEW TITLE:
THE GREEDY BABYMOUSE WHO WAS TOTALLY OBSESSED WITH GETTING A WHIZ BANG™.
WORKS FOR ME!

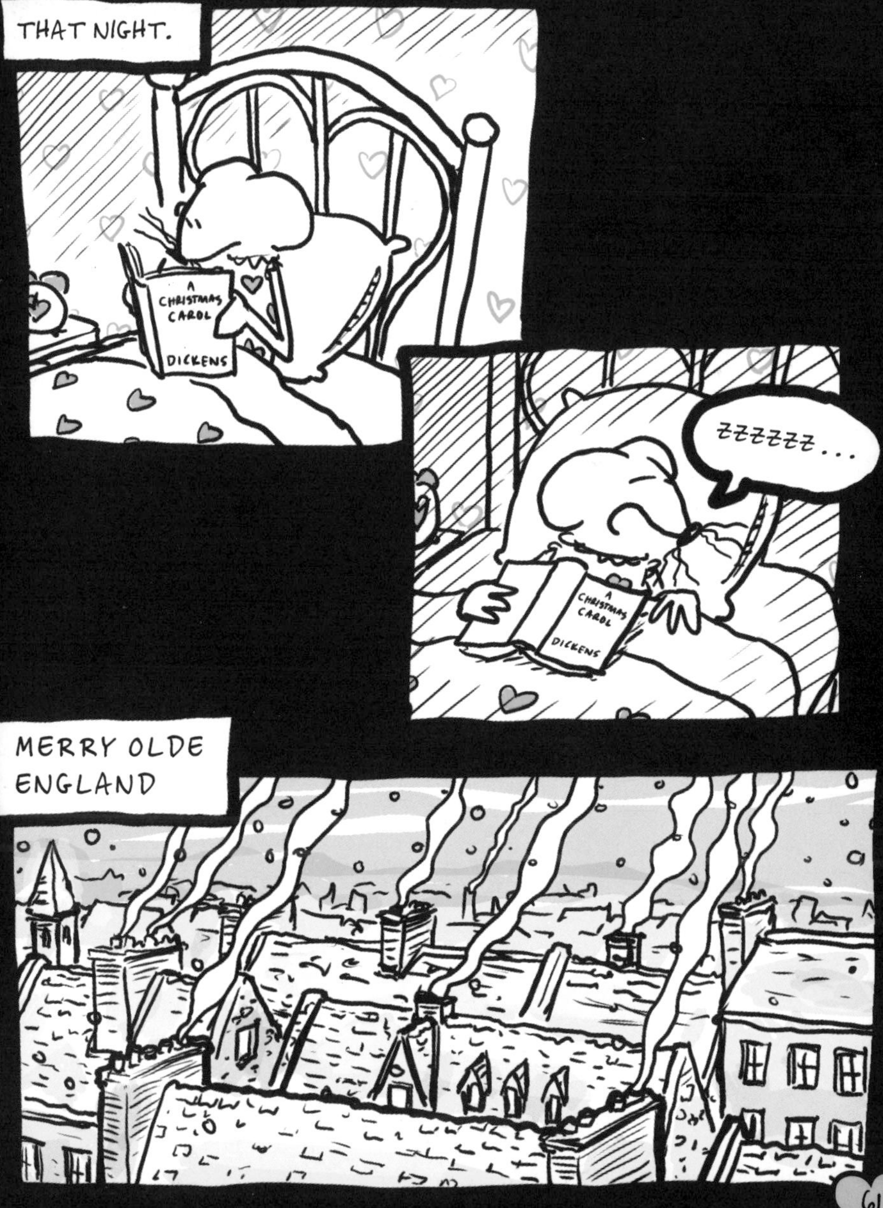
THAT NIGHT.
A CHRISTMAS CAROL
DICKENS
ZZZZZZ...
A CHRISTMAS CAROL
DICKENS
MERRY OLDE ENGLAND

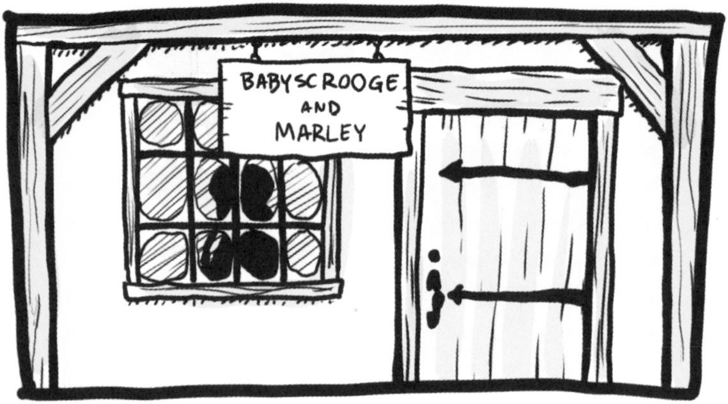
BABYSCROOGE AND MARLEY

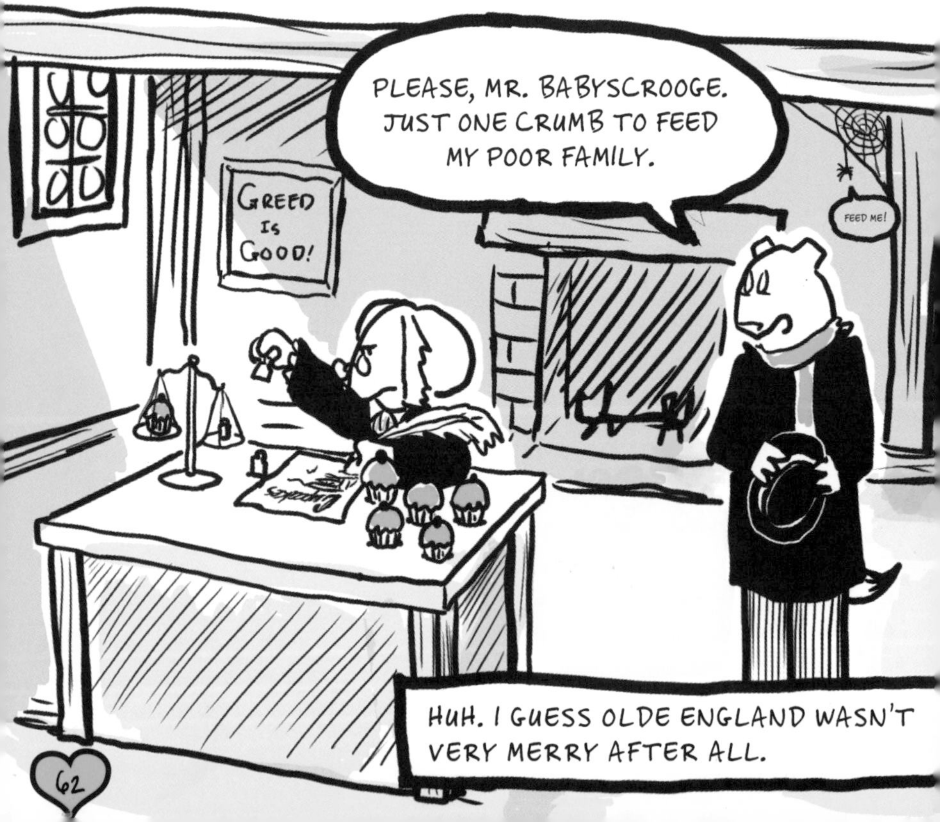
GREED IS GOOD!
PLEASE, MR. BABYSCROOGE. JUST ONE CRUMB TO FEED MY POOR FAMILY.
FEED ME!
HUH. I GUESS OLDE ENGLAND WASN'T VERY MERRY AFTER ALL.

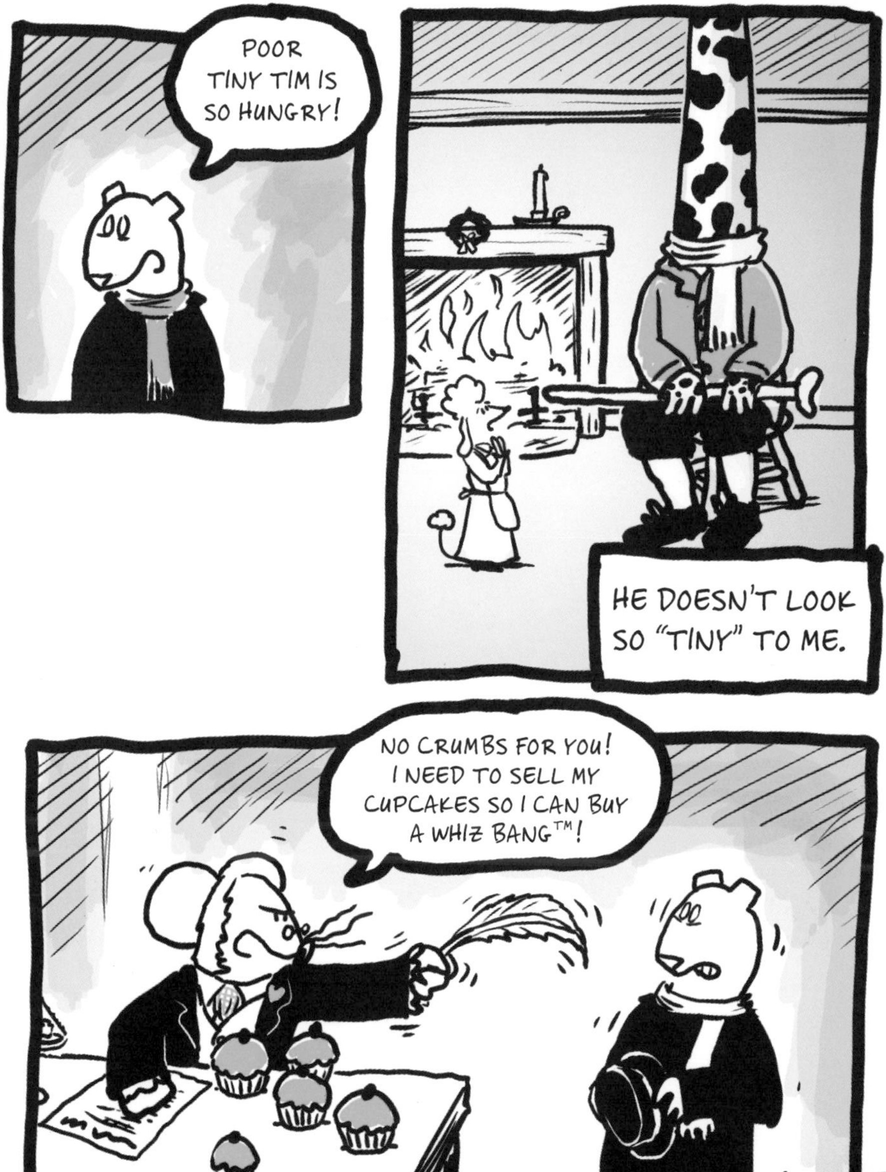
POOR TINY TIM IS SO HUNGRY!
HE DOESN'T LOOK SO "TINY" TO ME.
NO CRUMBS FOR YOU! I NEED TO SELL MY CUPCAKES SO I CAN BUY A WHIZ BANG™!

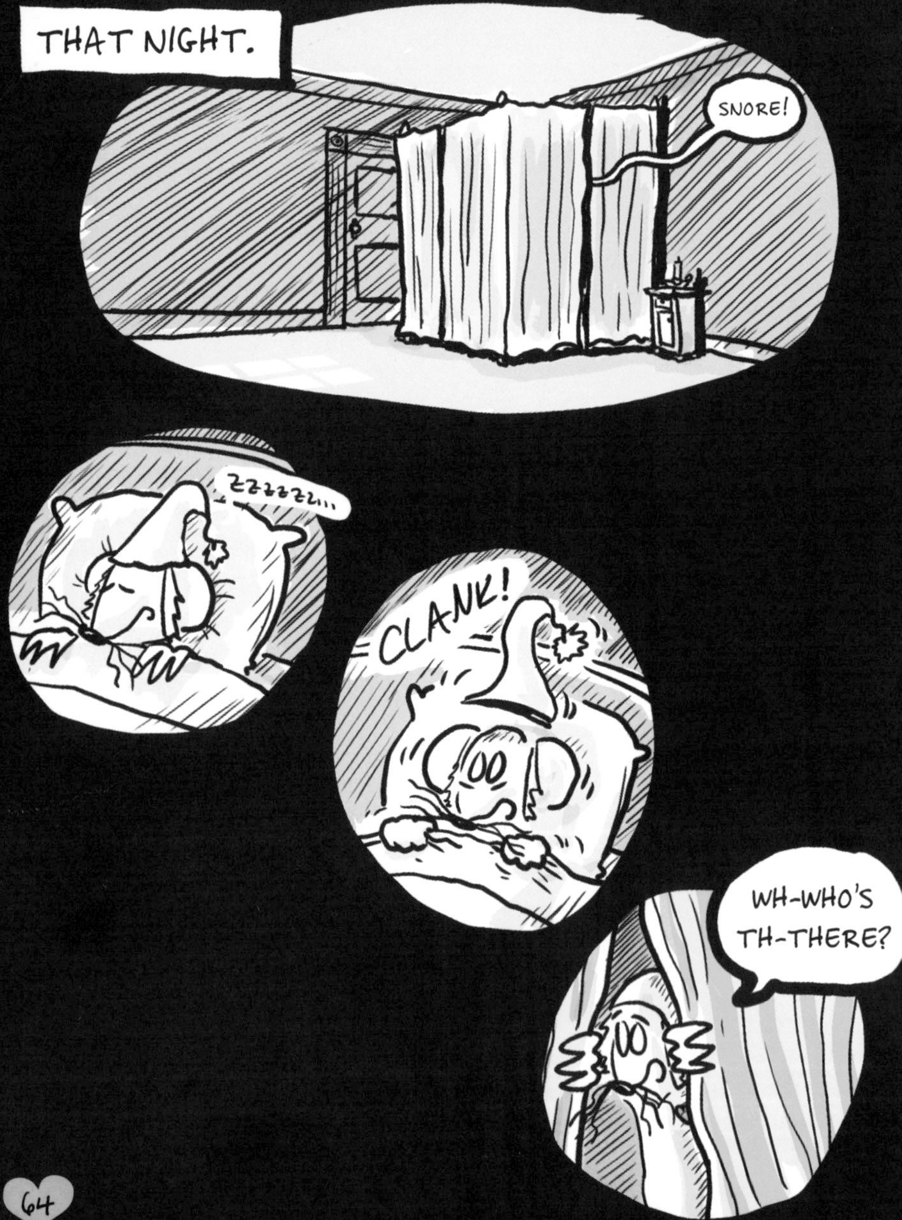
THAT NIGHT.
SNORE!
ZZZZZZZ...
CLANK!
WH-WHO'S TH-THERE?

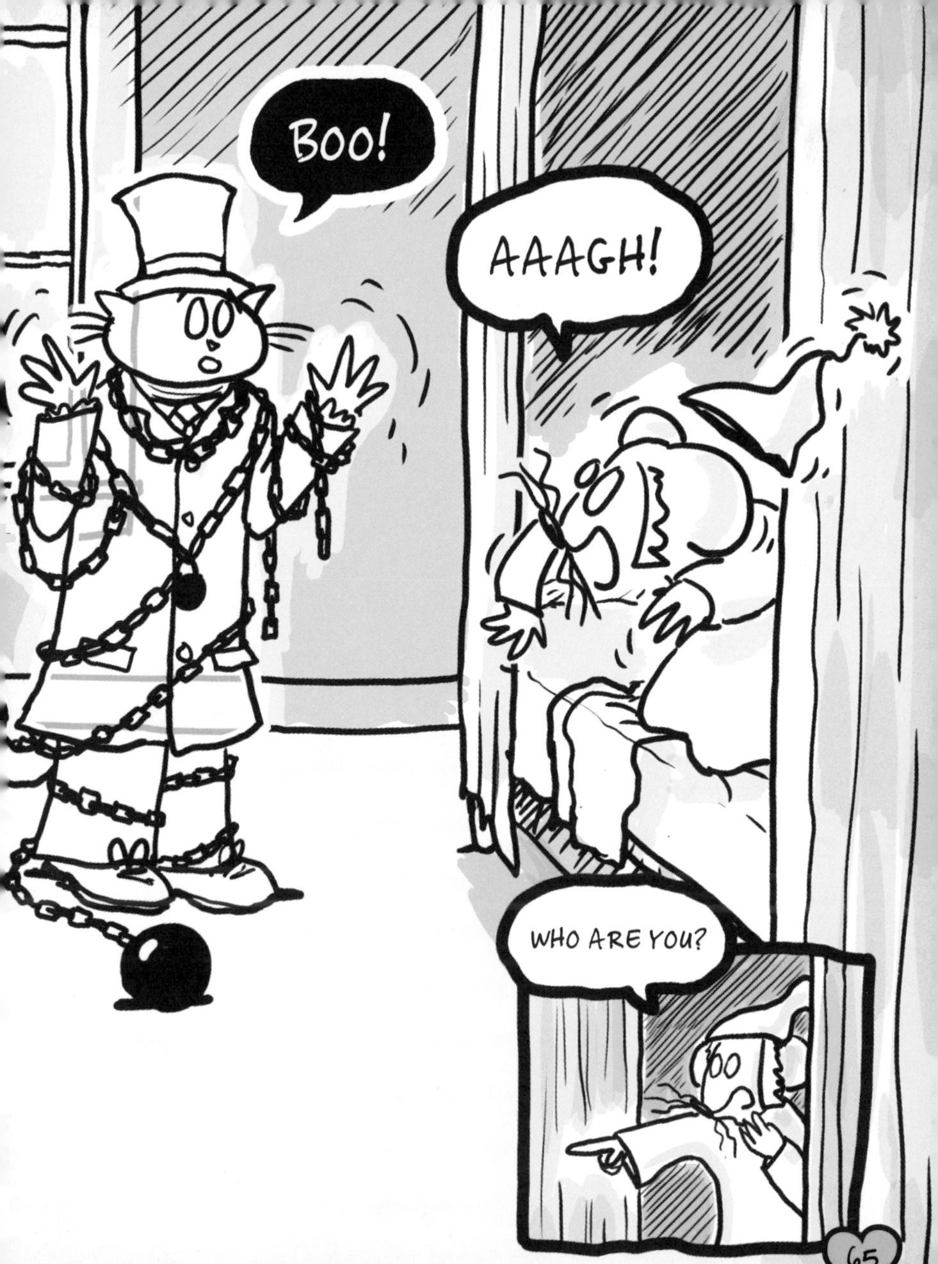
BOO!
AAAGH!
WHO ARE YOU?

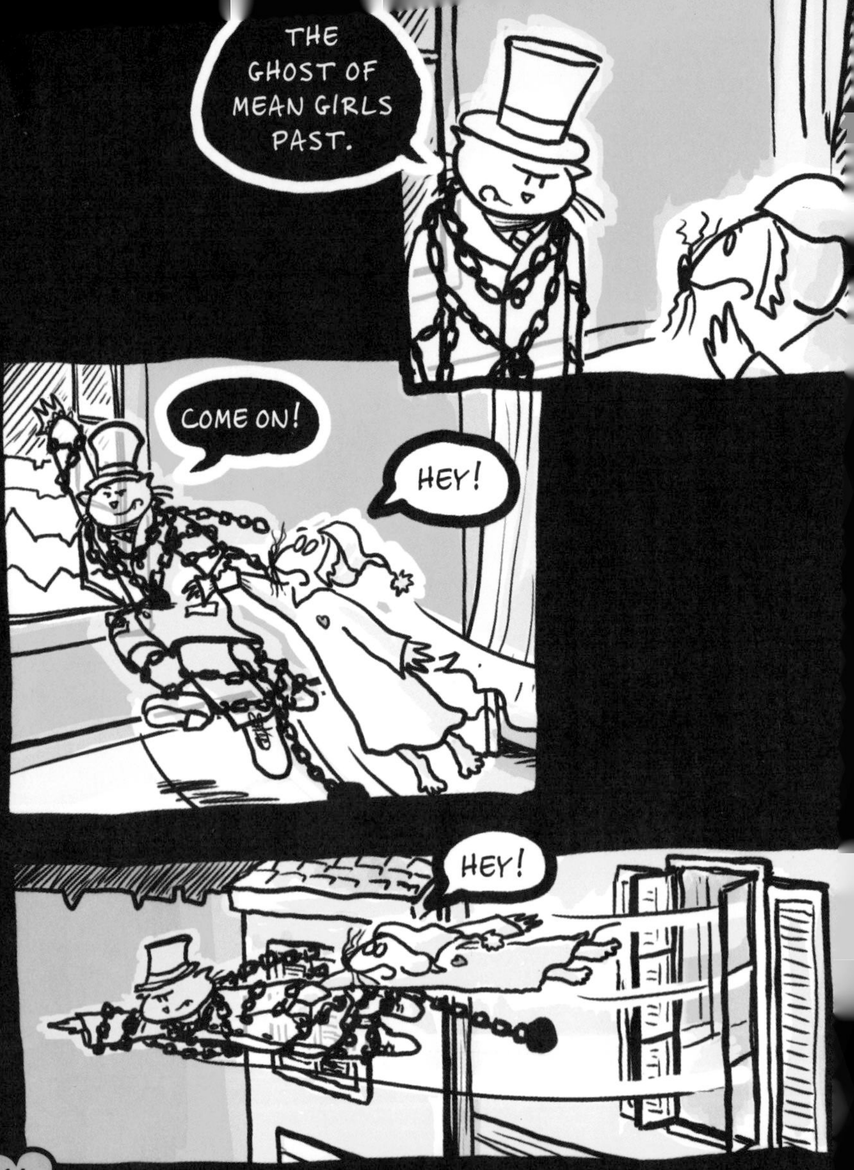

THE GHOST OF MEAN GIRLS PAST.
COME ON!
HEY!
HEY!

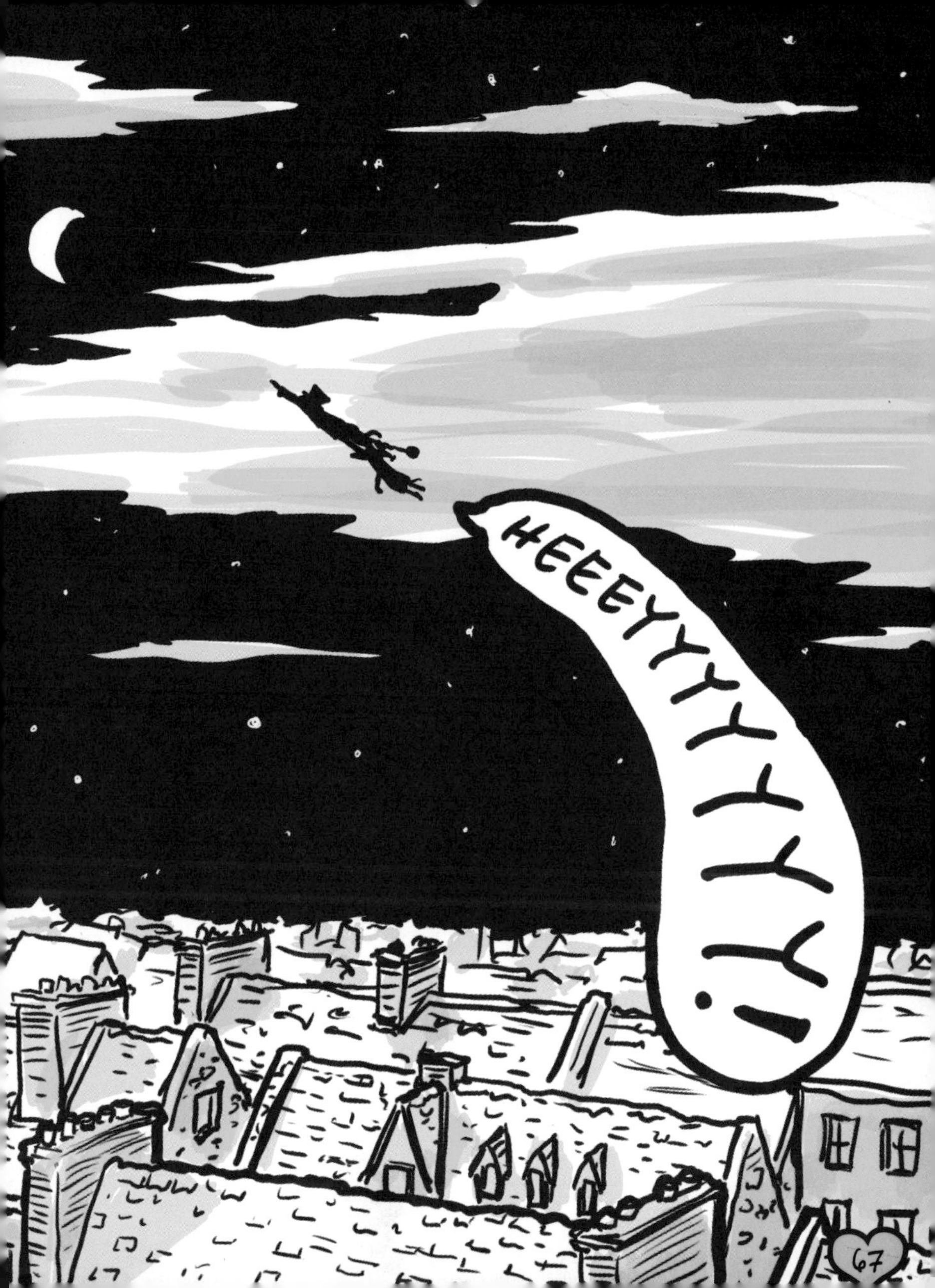
HEEEYYYYYYY!

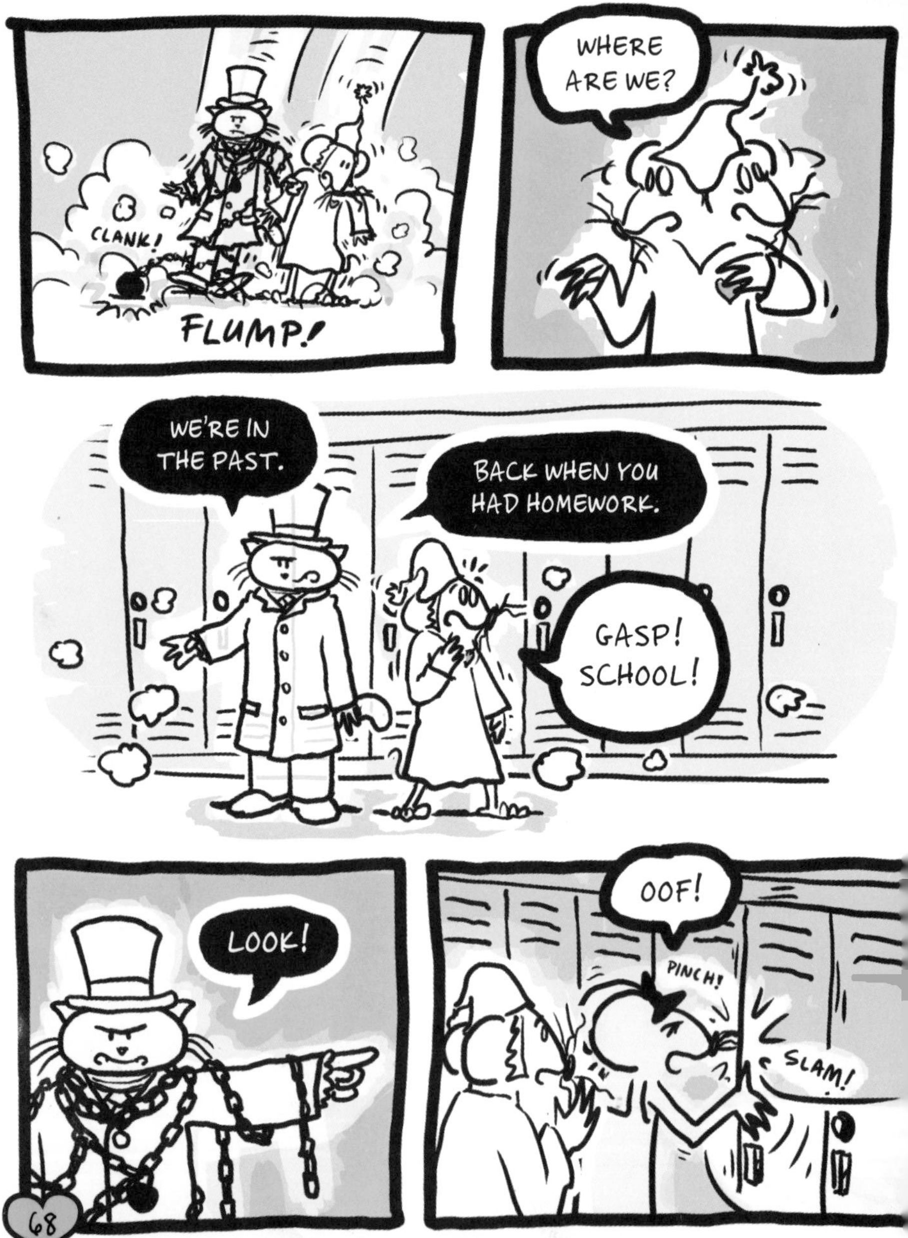
CLANK!
FLUMP!
WHERE ARE WE?
WE'RE IN THE PAST.
BACK WHEN YOU HAD HOMEWORK.
GASP! SCHOOL!
LOOK!
OOF!
PINCH!
SLAM!

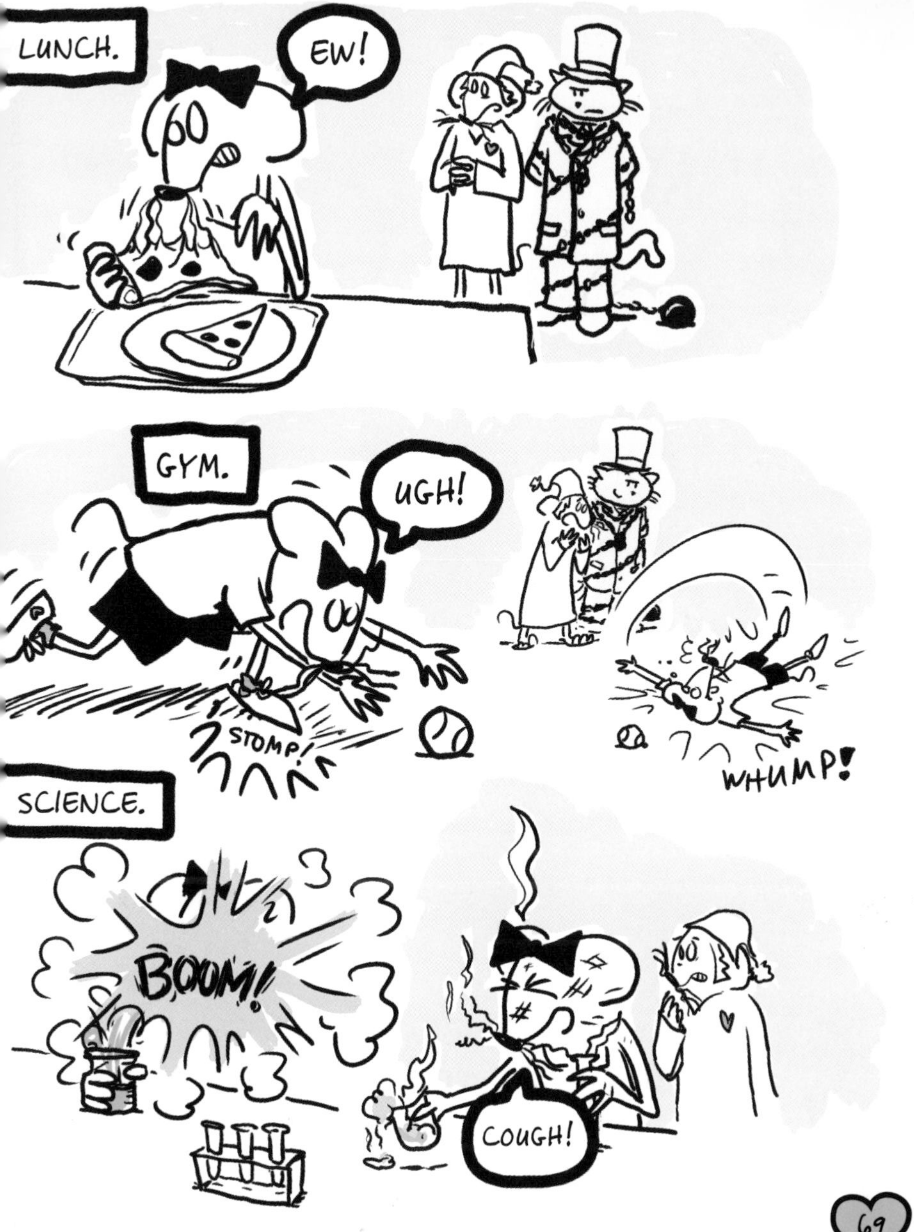
LUNCH.
EW!
GYM.
UGH!
STOMP!
WHUMP!
SCIENCE.
BOOM!
COUGH!

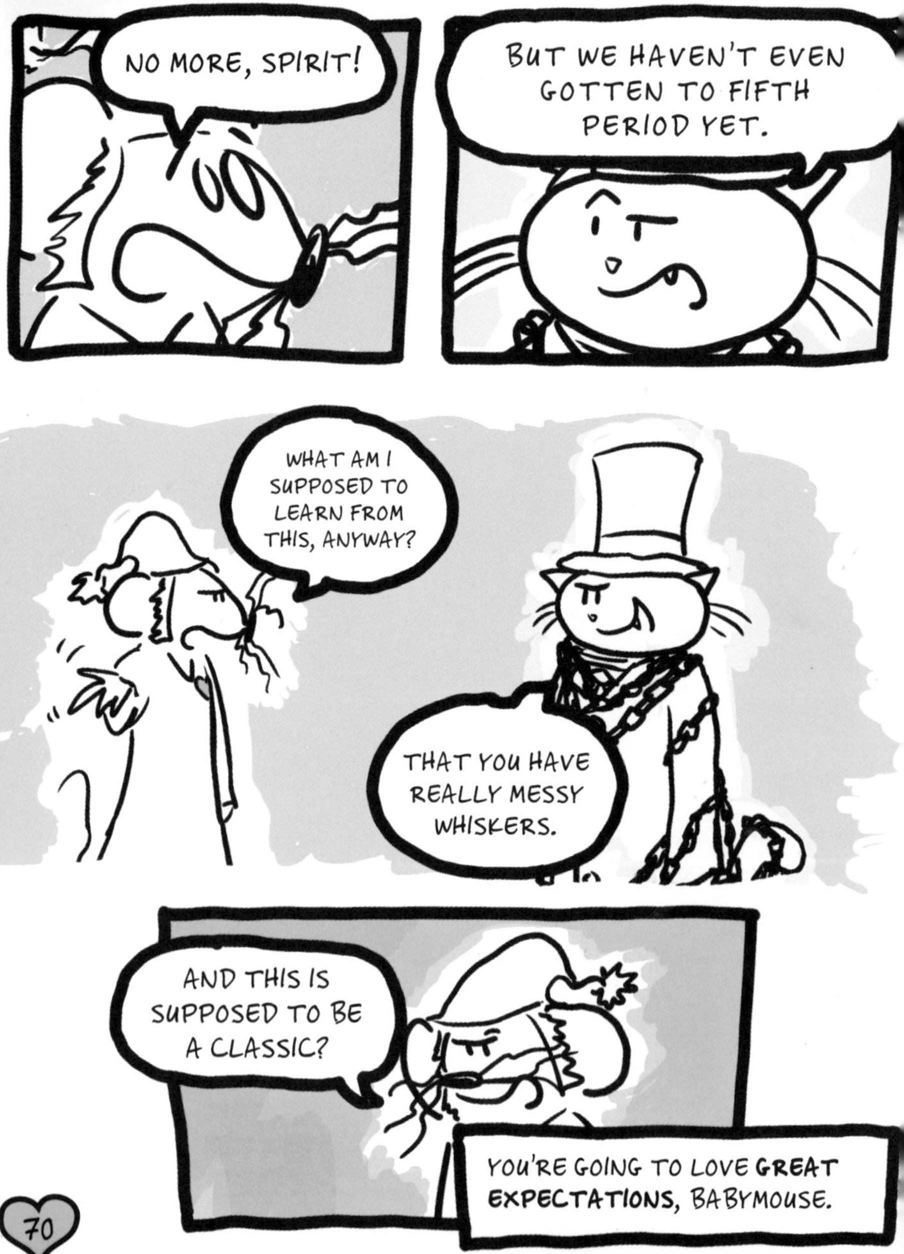
NO MORE, SPIRIT!
BUT WE HAVEN'T EVEN GOTTEN TO FIFTH PERIOD YET.
WHAT AM I SUPPOSED TO LEARN FROM THIS, ANYWAY?
THAT YOU HAVE REALLY MESSY WHISKERS.
AND THIS IS SUPPOSED TO BE A CLASSIC?
YOU'RE GOING TO LOVE **GREAT EXPECTATIONS**, BABYMOUSE.

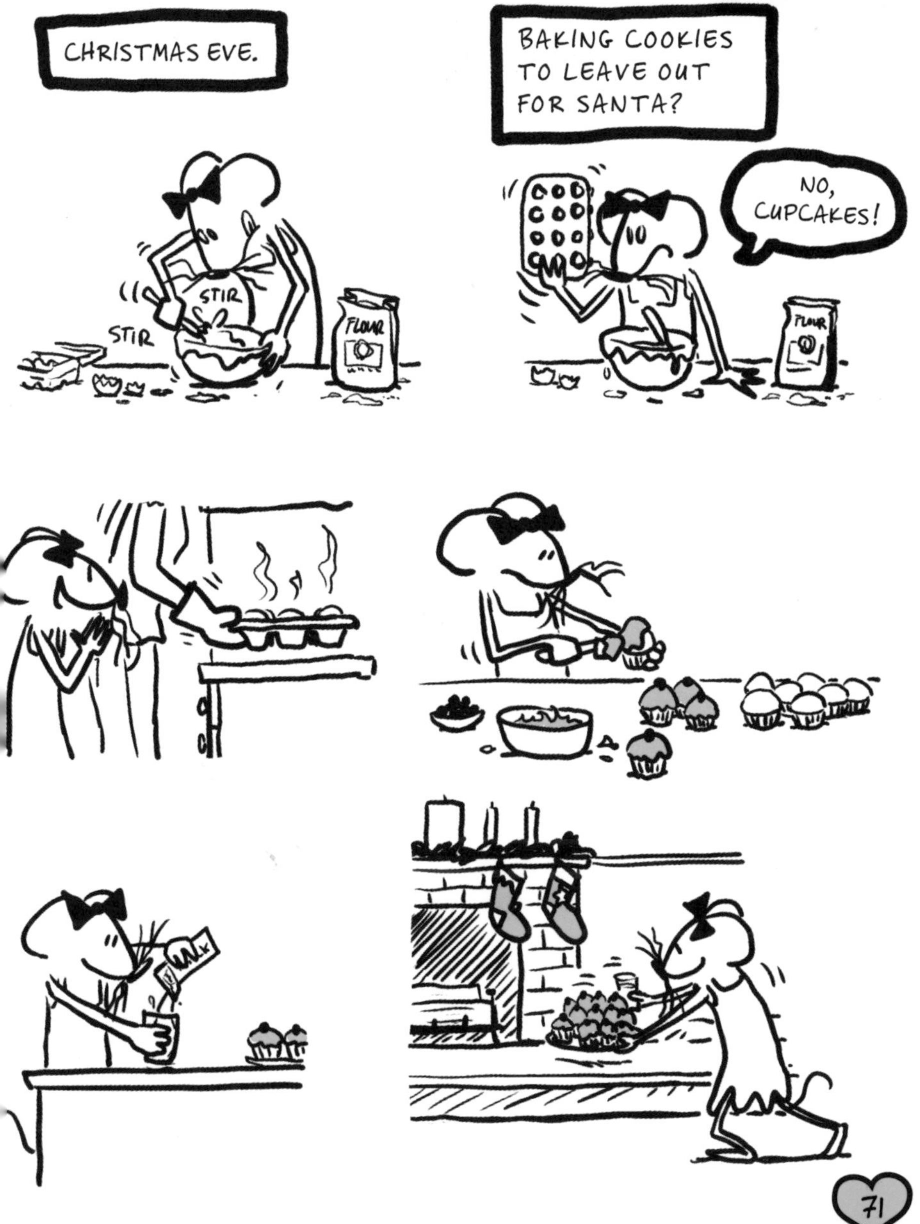
CHRISTMAS EVE.
STIR
STIR
FLOUR
BAKING COOKIES TO LEAVE OUT FOR SANTA?
NO, CUPCAKES!
FLOUR

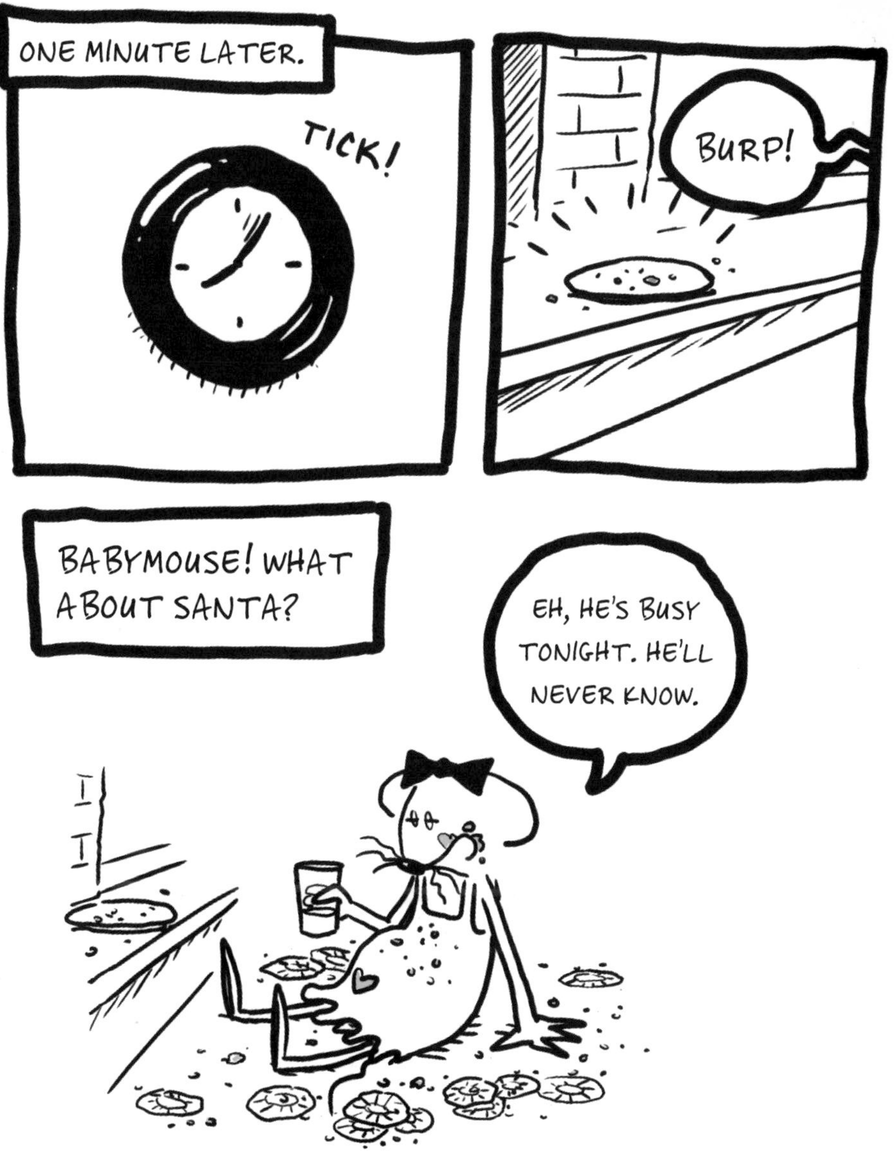
ONE MINUTE LATER.
TICK!
BURP!
BABYMOUSE! WHAT ABOUT SANTA?
EH, HE'S BUSY TONIGHT. HE'LL NEVER KNOW.

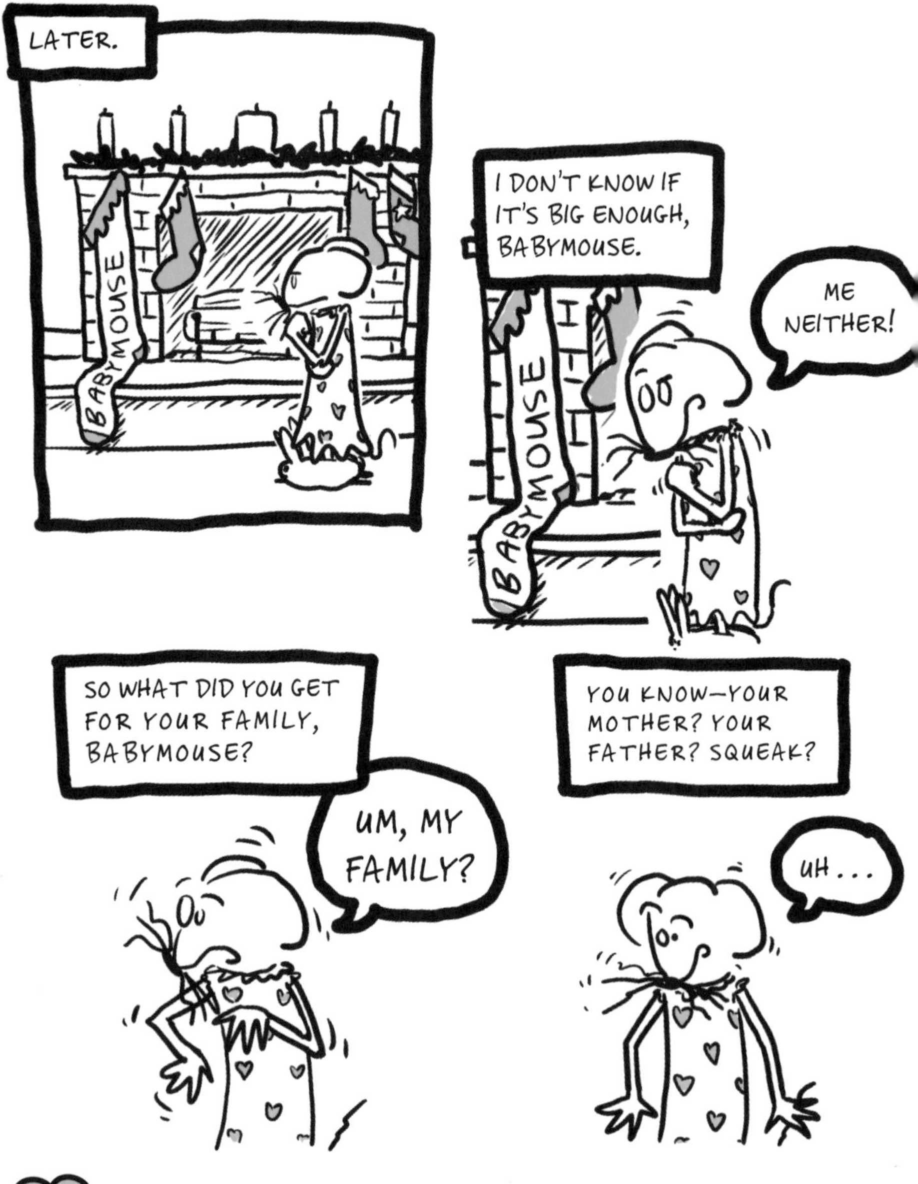
LATER.
BABYMOUSE
I DON'T KNOW IF IT'S BIG ENOUGH, BABYMOUSE.
ME NEITHER!
BABYMOUSE
SO WHAT DID YOU GET FOR YOUR FAMILY, BABYMOUSE?
UM, MY FAMILY?
YOU KNOW—YOUR MOTHER? YOUR FATHER? SQUEAK?
UH . . .

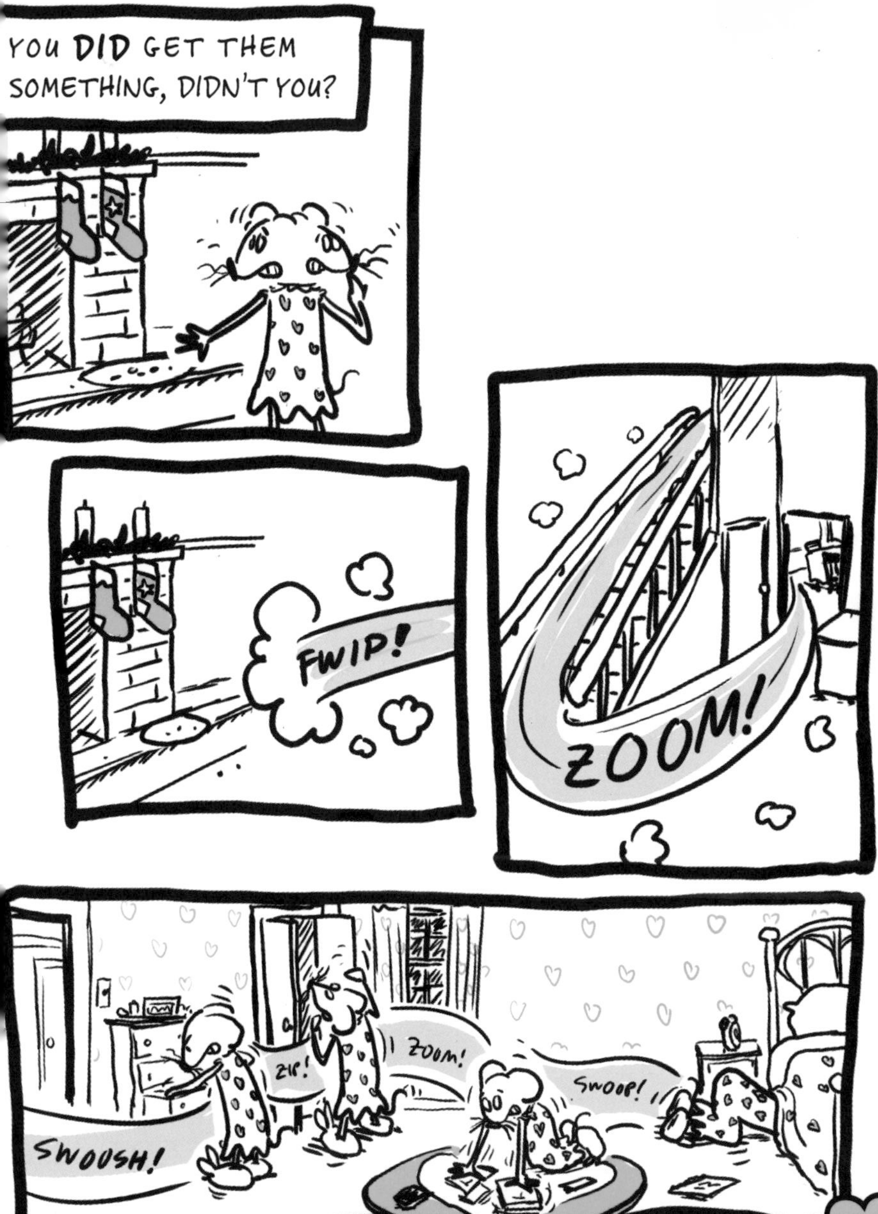
YOU DID GET THEM SOMETHING, DIDN'T YOU?
FWIP!
ZOOM!
SWOOSH!
ZIP!
ZOOM!
SWOOP!

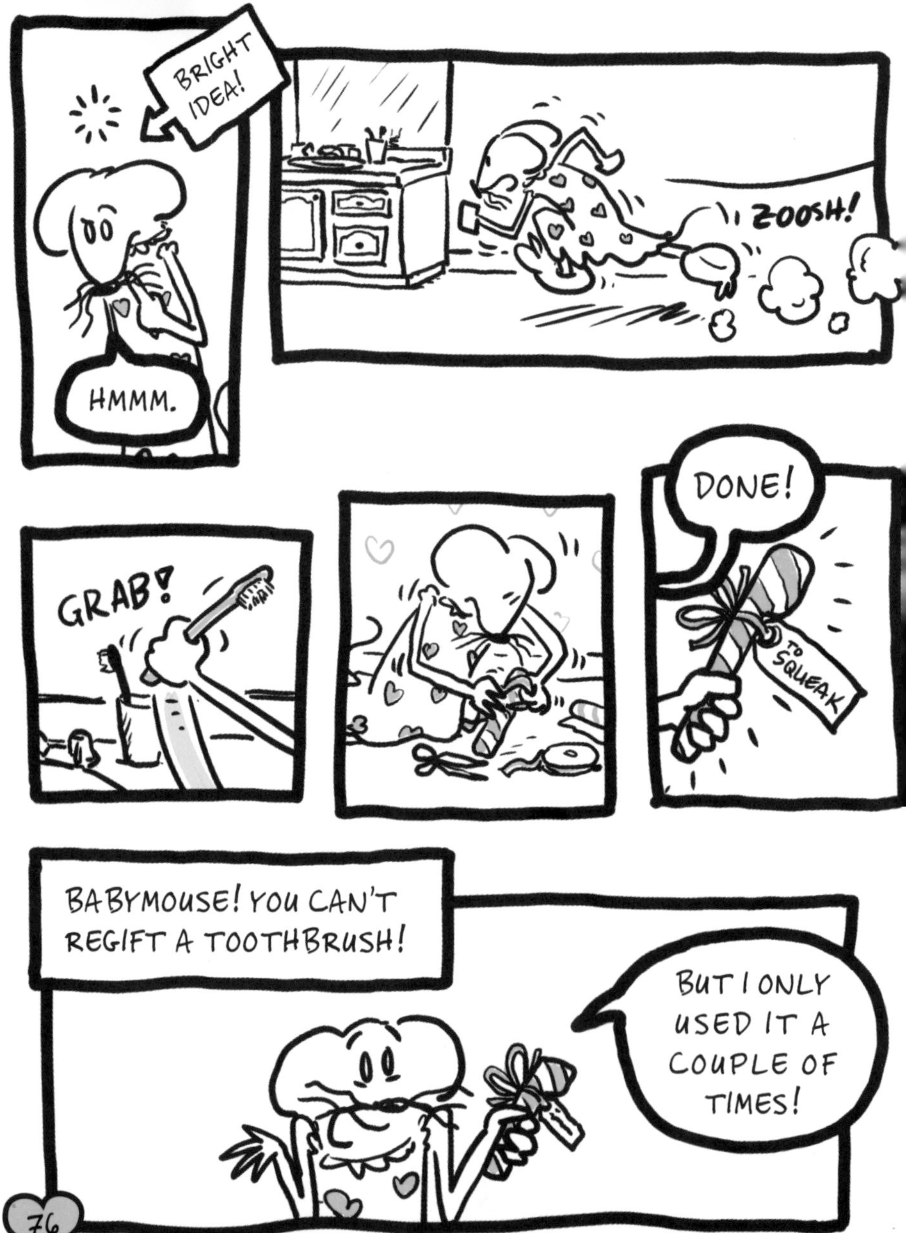
BRIGHT IDEA!
HMMM.
ZOOSH!
GRAB!
DONE!
TO SQUEAK
BABYMOUSE! YOU CAN'T REGIFT A TOOTHBRUSH!
BUT I ONLY USED IT A COUPLE OF TIMES!

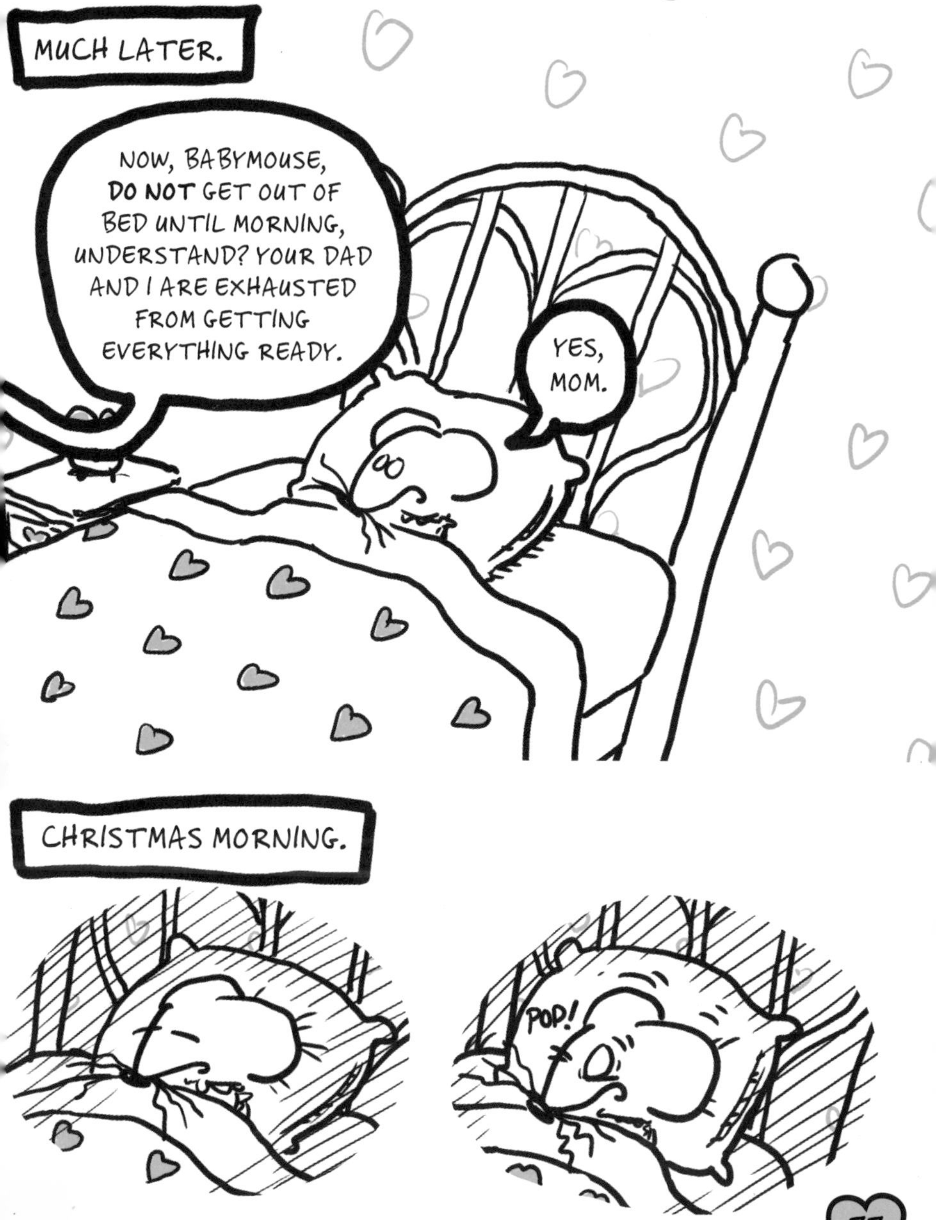
MUCH LATER.
NOW, BABYMOUSE, DO NOT GET OUT OF BED UNTIL MORNING, UNDERSTAND? YOUR DAD AND I ARE EXHAUSTED FROM GETTING EVERYTHING READY.
YES, MOM.
CHRISTMAS MORNING.
POP!

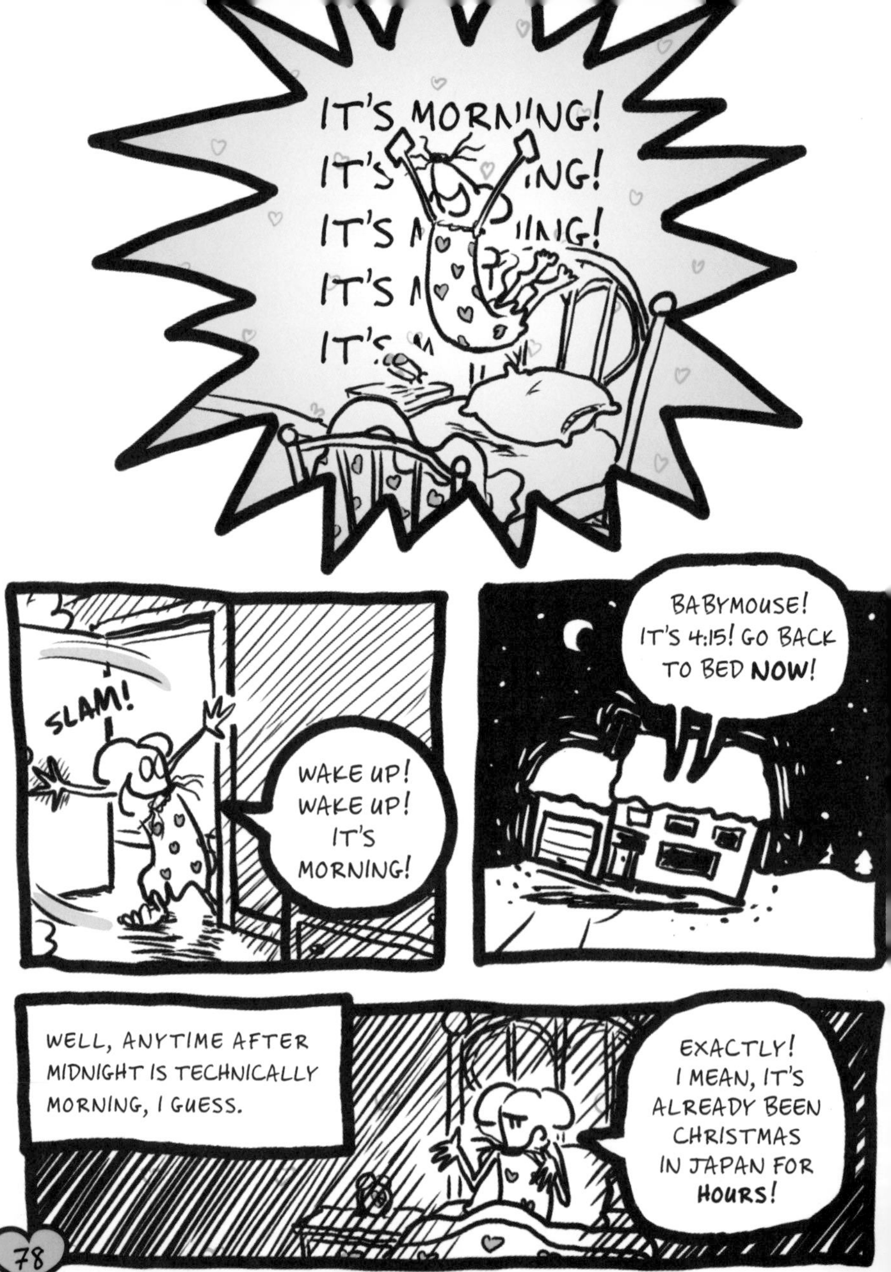
IT'S MORNING!
IT'S ING!
IT'S INING!
IT'S
IT'S
SLAM!
WAKE UP! WAKE UP! IT'S MORNING!
BABYMOUSE! IT'S 4:15! GO BACK TO BED **NOW**!
WELL, ANYTIME AFTER MIDNIGHT IS TECHNICALLY MORNING, I GUESS.
EXACTLY! I MEAN, IT'S ALREADY BEEN CHRISTMAS IN JAPAN FOR **HOURS**!

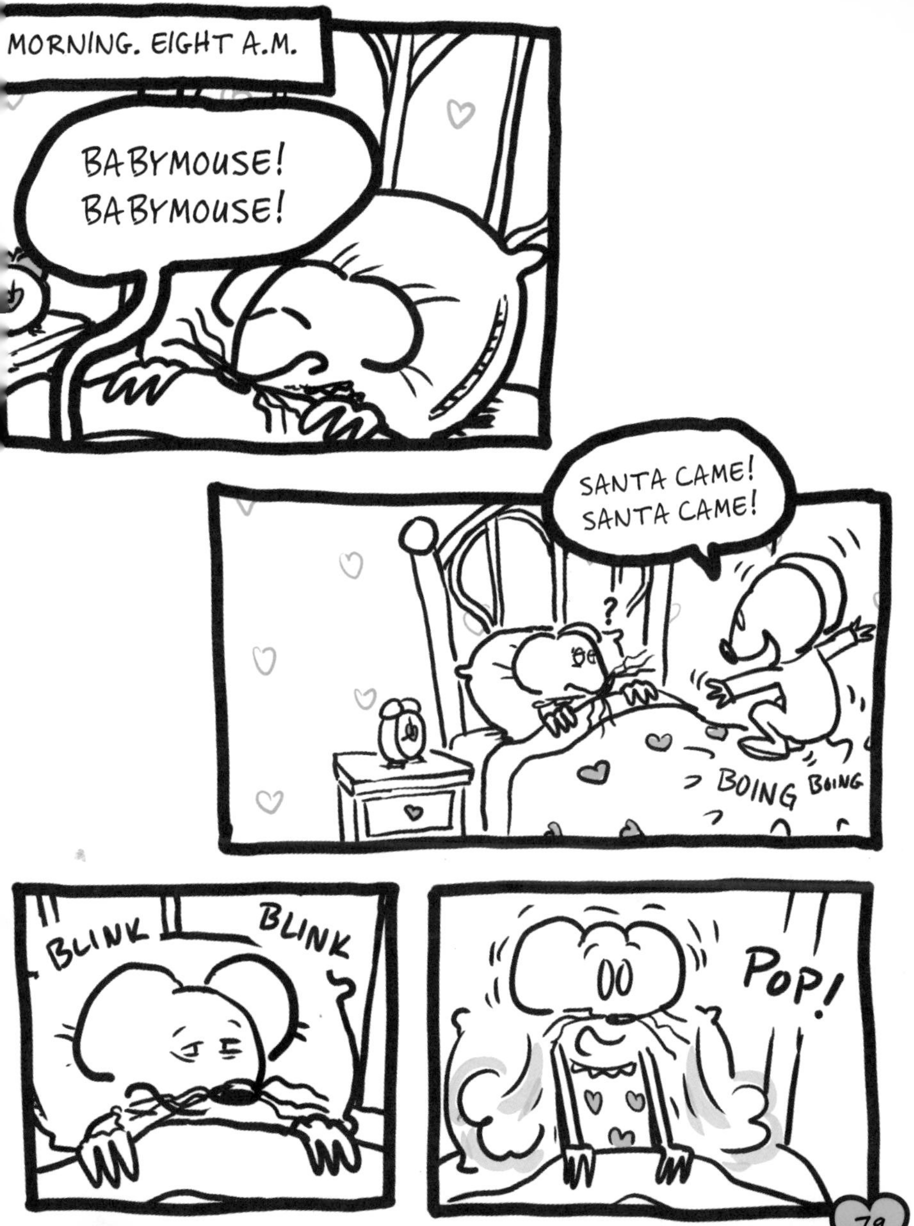
MORNING. EIGHT A.M.
BABYMOUSE! BABYMOUSE!
SANTA CAME! SANTA CAME!
BOING BOING
BLINK BLINK
POP!

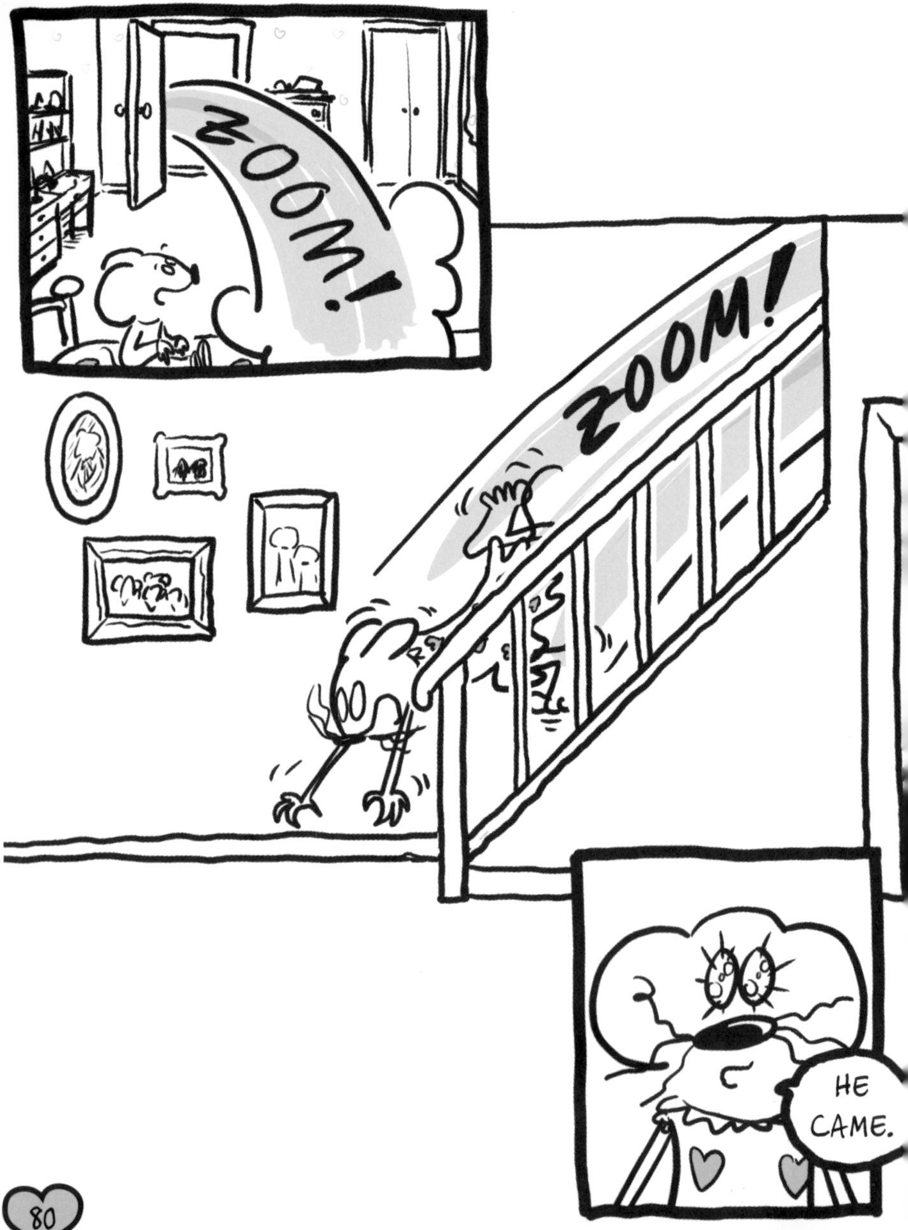
ZOOM!
ZOOM!
HE CAME.

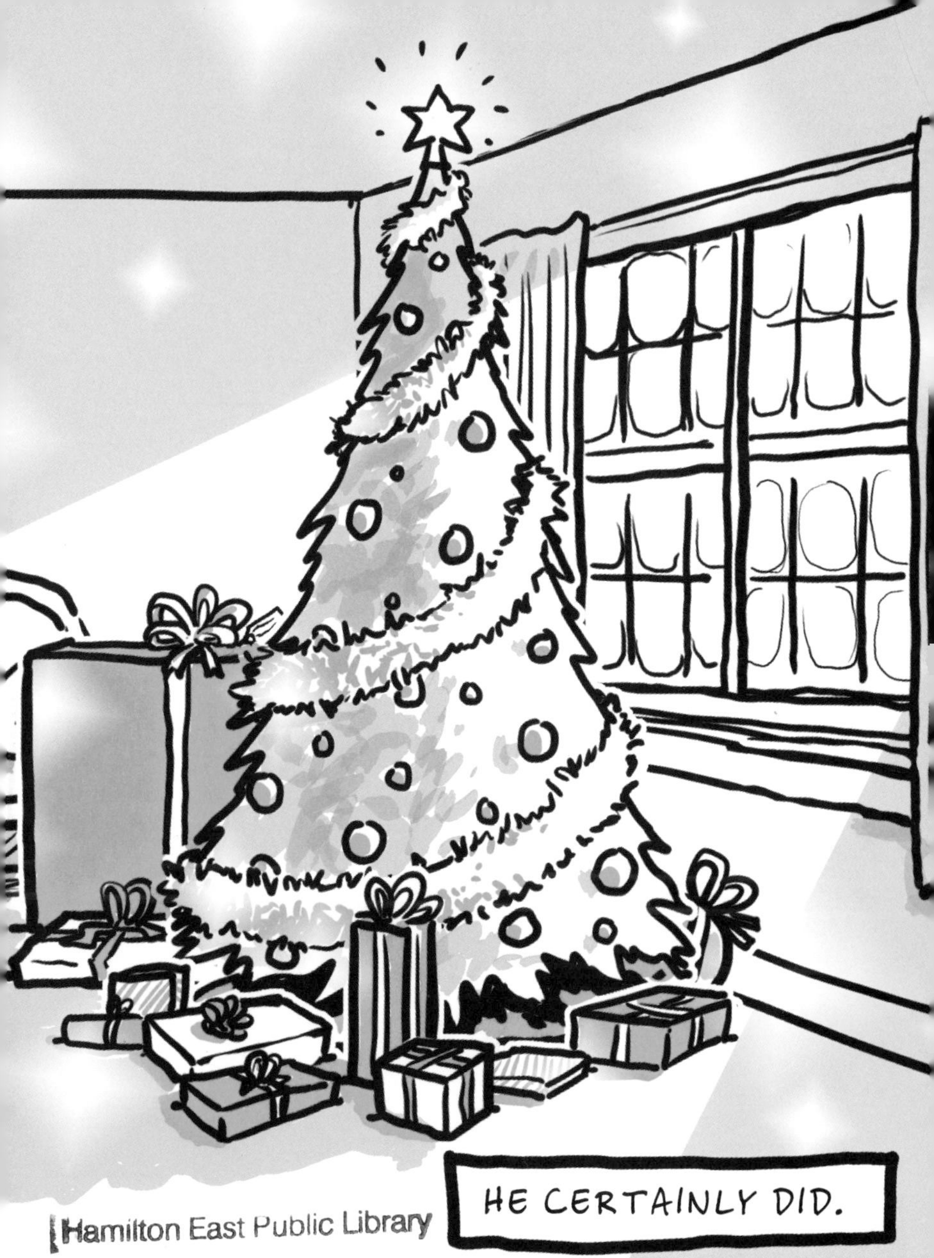
HE CERTAINLY DID.

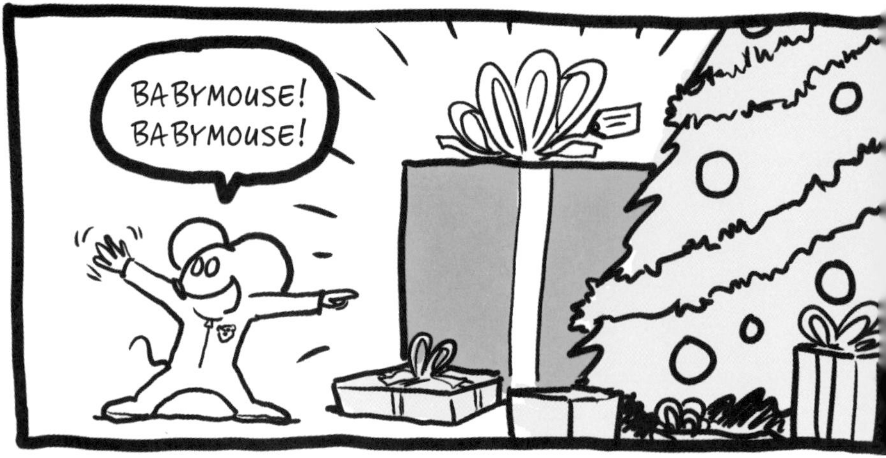
BABYMOUSE! BABYMOUSE!

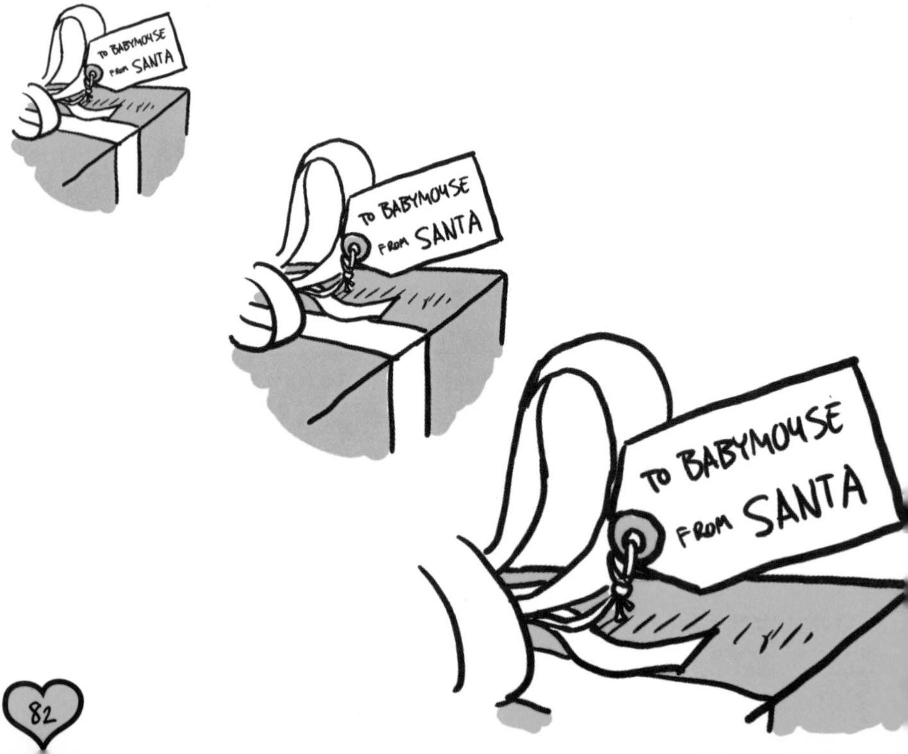
TO BABYMOUSE FROM SANTA
TO BABYMOUSE FROM SANTA
TO BABYMOUSE FROM SANTA

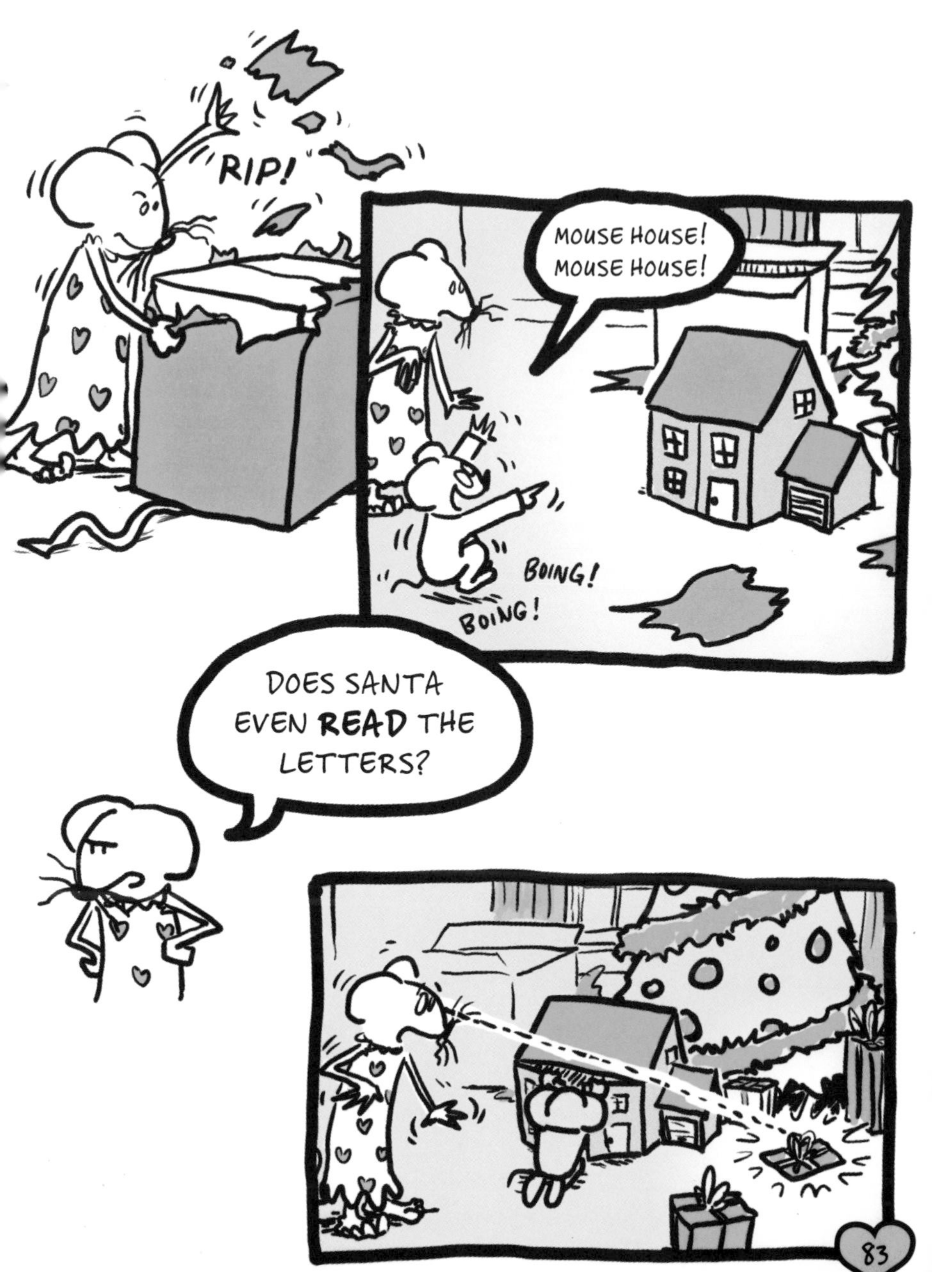
RIP!
MOUSE HOUSE! MOUSE HOUSE!
BOING!
BOING!
DOES SANTA EVEN **READ** THE LETTERS?

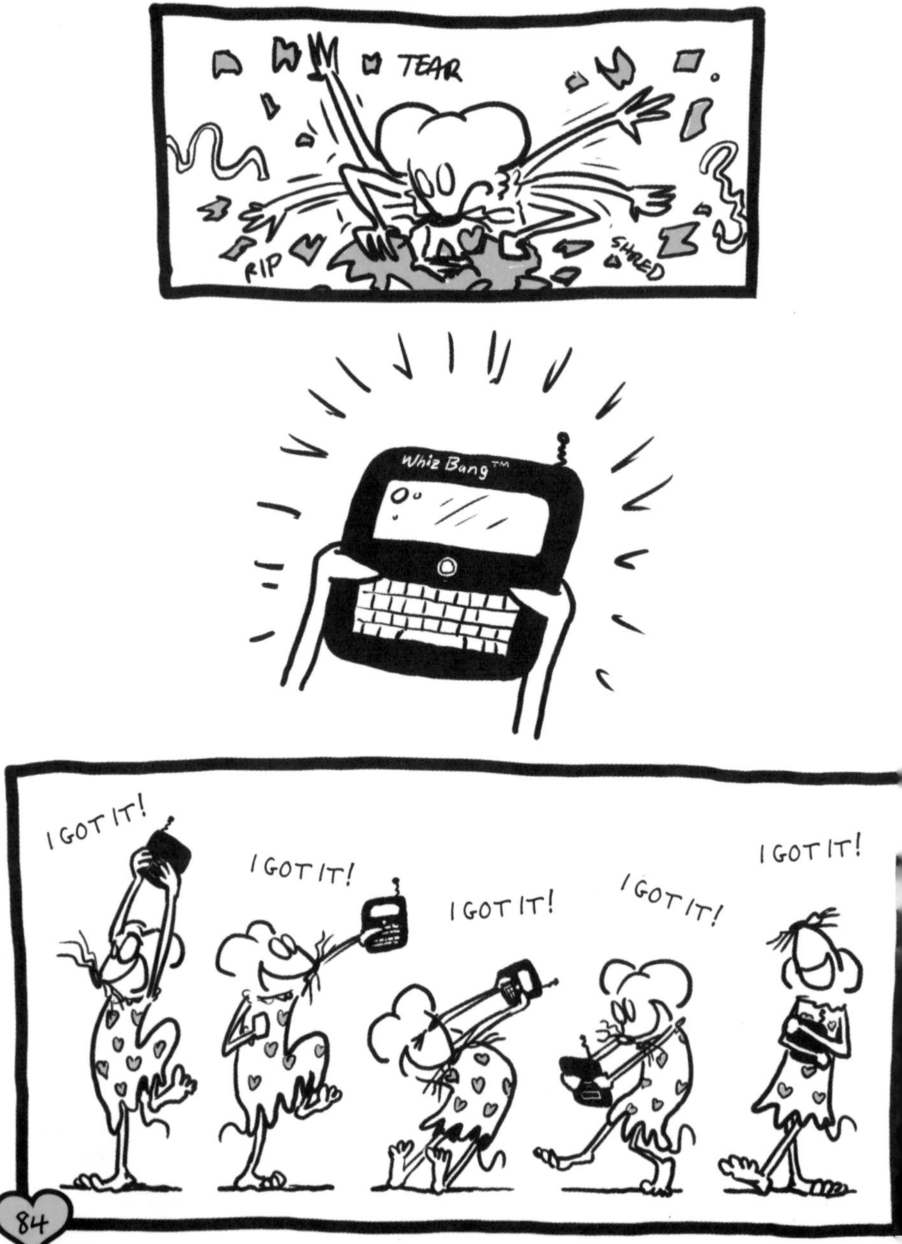
TEAR
RIP
SHRED
Whiz Bang™
I GOT IT!
I GOT IT!
I GOT IT!
I GOT IT!
I GOT IT!

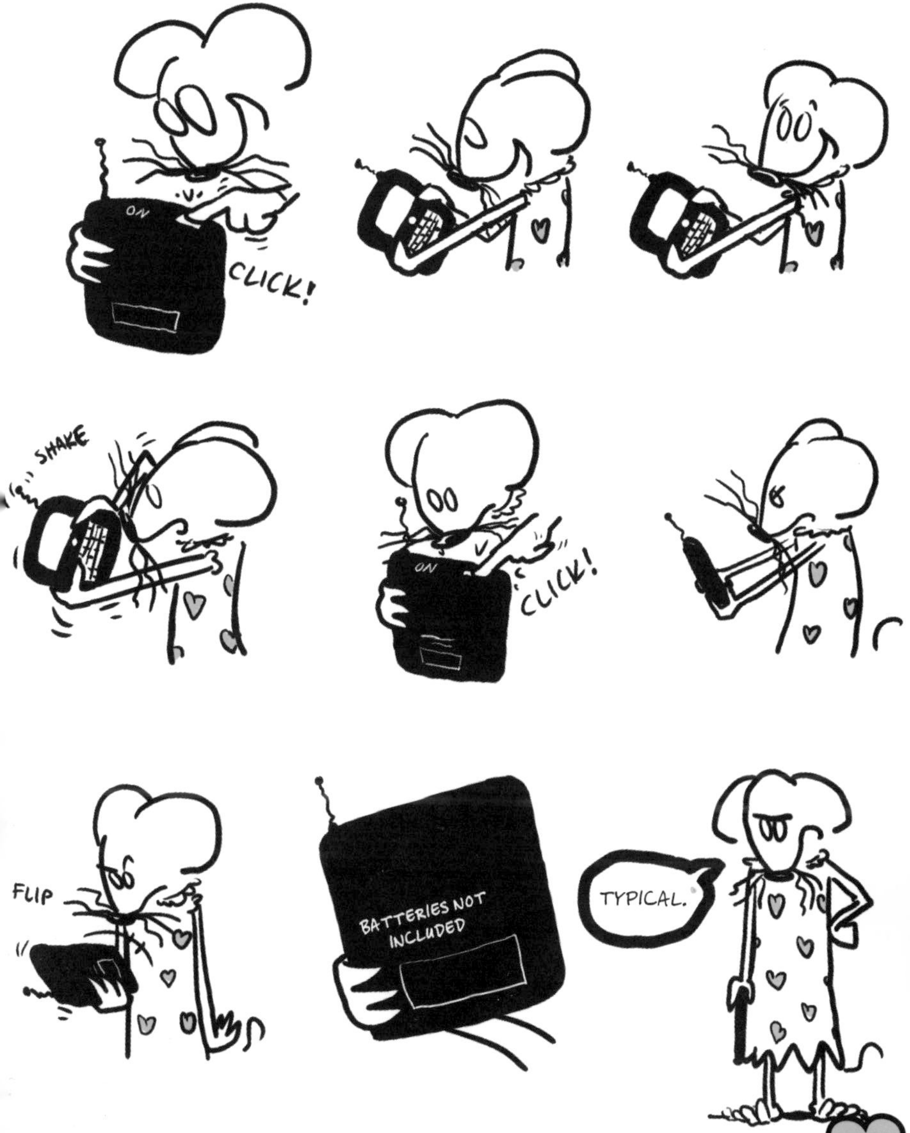
ON
CLICK!
SHAKE
ON
CLICK!
FLIP
BATTERIES NOT INCLUDED
TYPICAL.

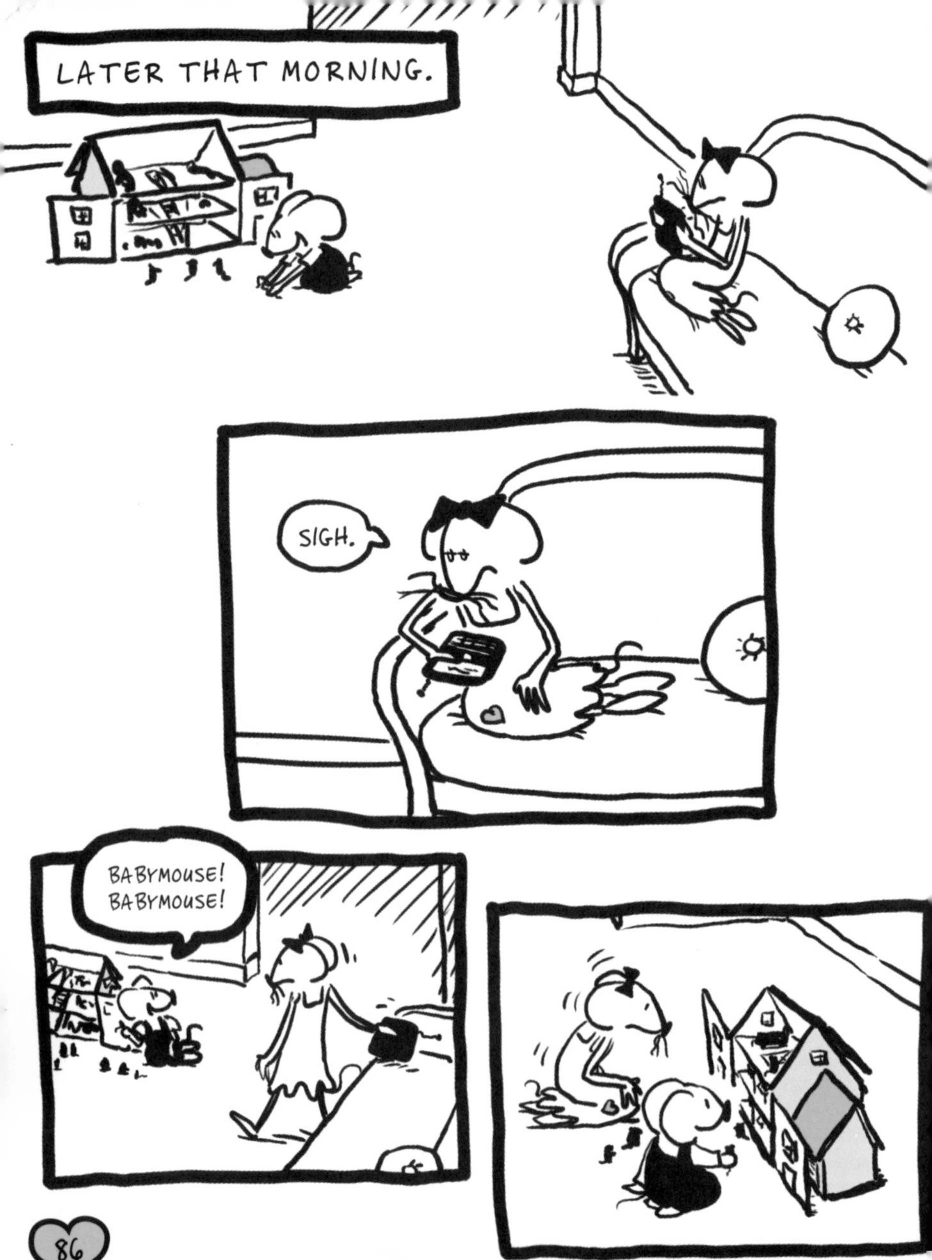
LATER THAT MORNING.
SIGH.
BABYMOUSE! BABYMOUSE!

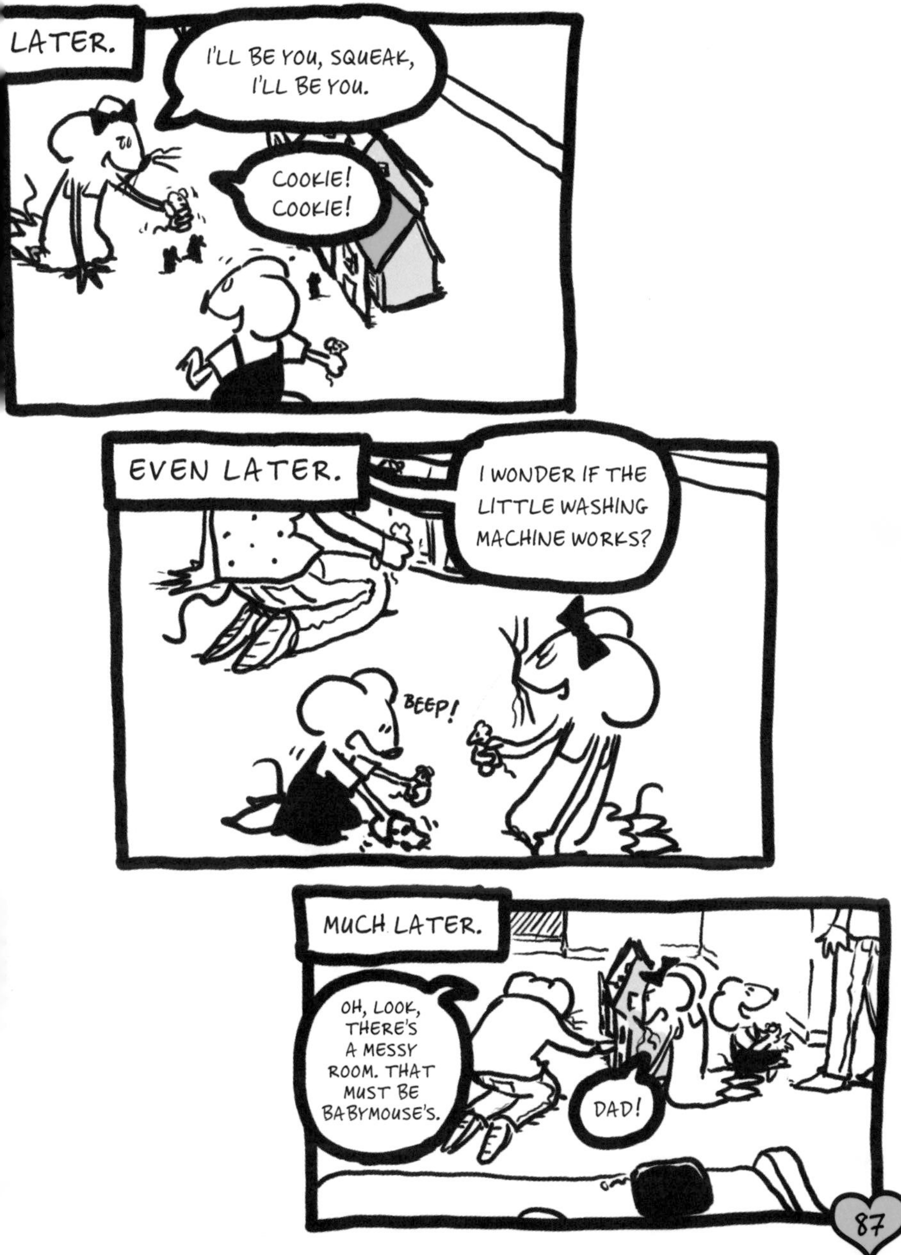
LATER.
I'LL BE YOU, SQUEAK, I'LL BE YOU.
COOKIE! COOKIE!
EVEN LATER.
I WONDER IF THE LITTLE WASHING MACHINE WORKS?
BEEP!
MUCH LATER.
OH, LOOK, THERE'S A MESSY ROOM. THAT MUST BE BABYMOUSE'S.
DAD!

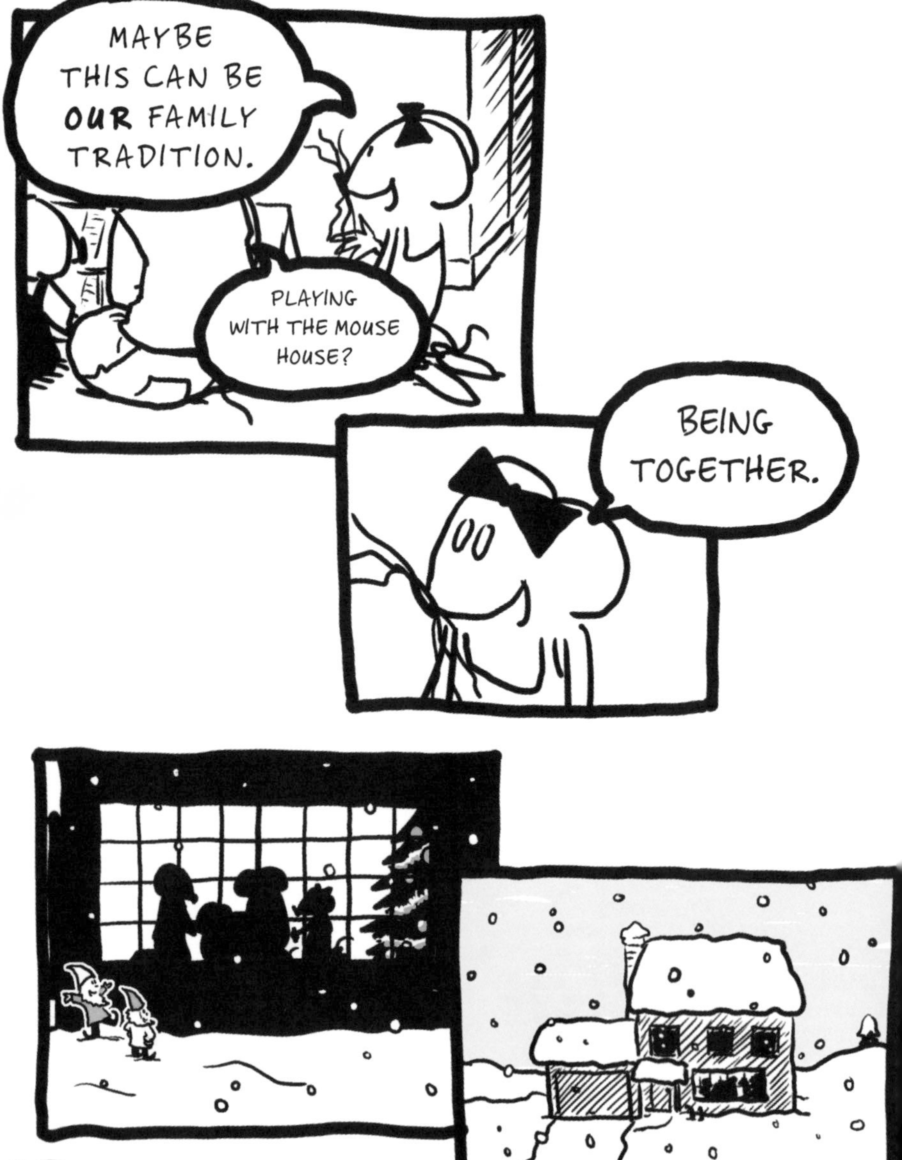
MAYBE THIS CAN BE **OUR** FAMILY TRADITION.
PLAYING WITH THE MOUSE HOUSE?
BEING TOGETHER.

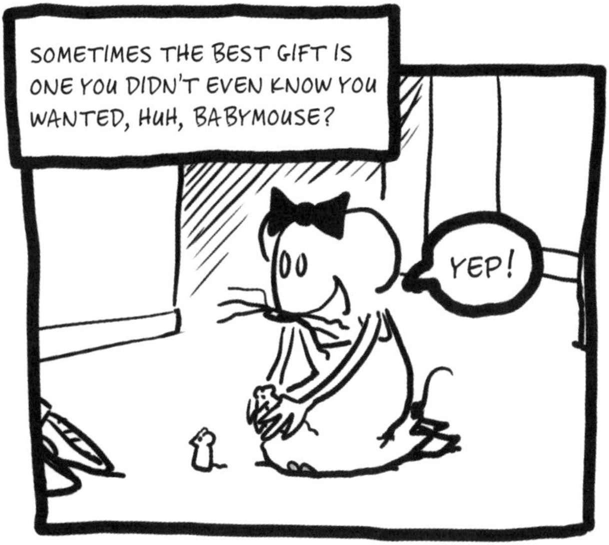
SOMETIMES THE BEST GIFT IS ONE YOU DIDN'T EVEN KNOW YOU WANTED, HUH, BABYMOUSE?
YEP!

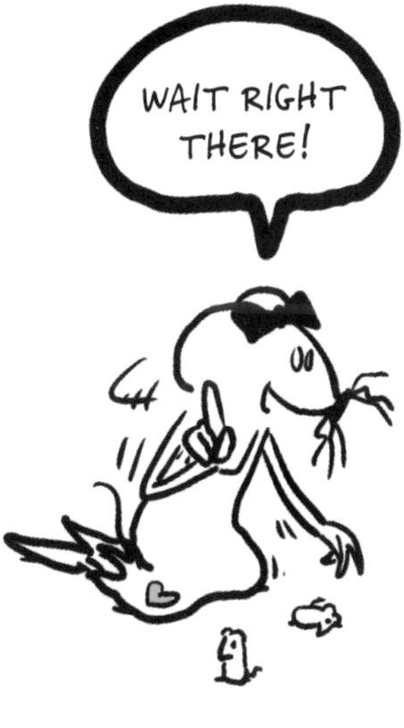
WAIT RIGHT THERE!

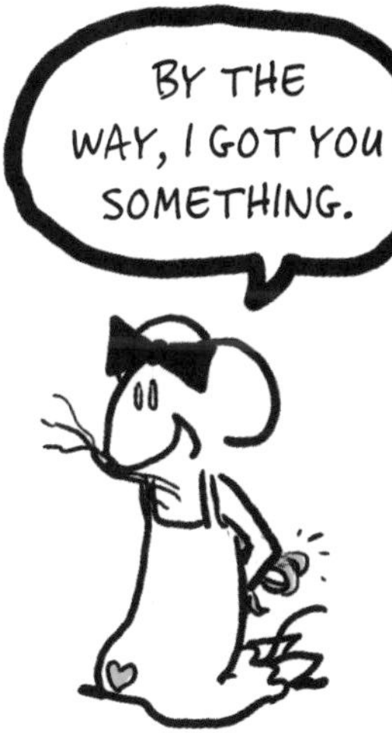
BY THE WAY, I GOT YOU SOMETHING.

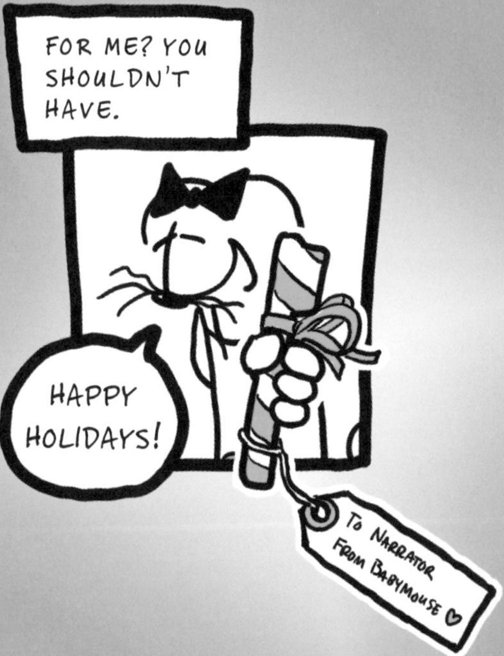
FOR ME? YOU SHOULDN'T HAVE.
HAPPY HOLIDAYS!
TO NARRATOR FROM BABYMOUSE ♥

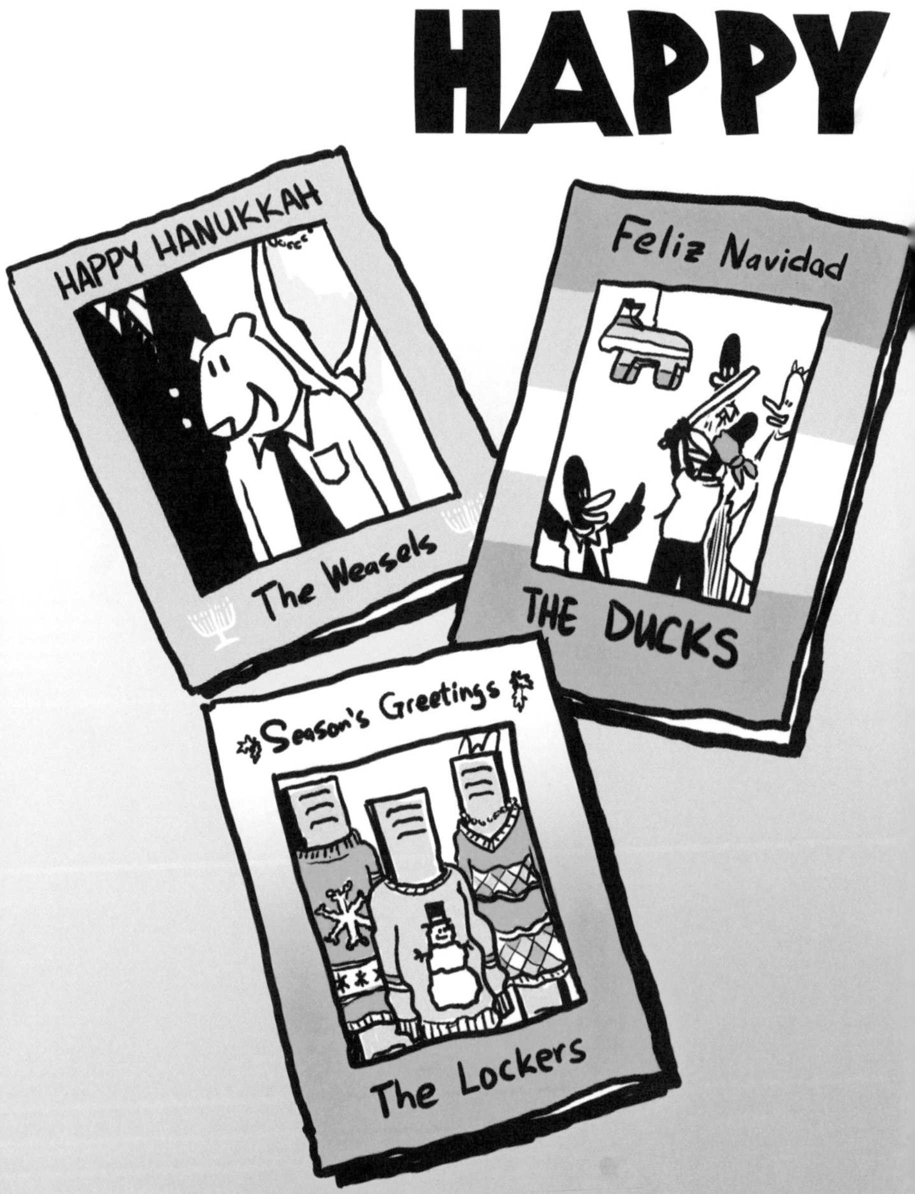
HAPPY
HAPPY HANUKKAH
The Weasels
Feliz Navidad
THE DUCKS
Season's Greetings
The Lockers

HOLIDAYS!

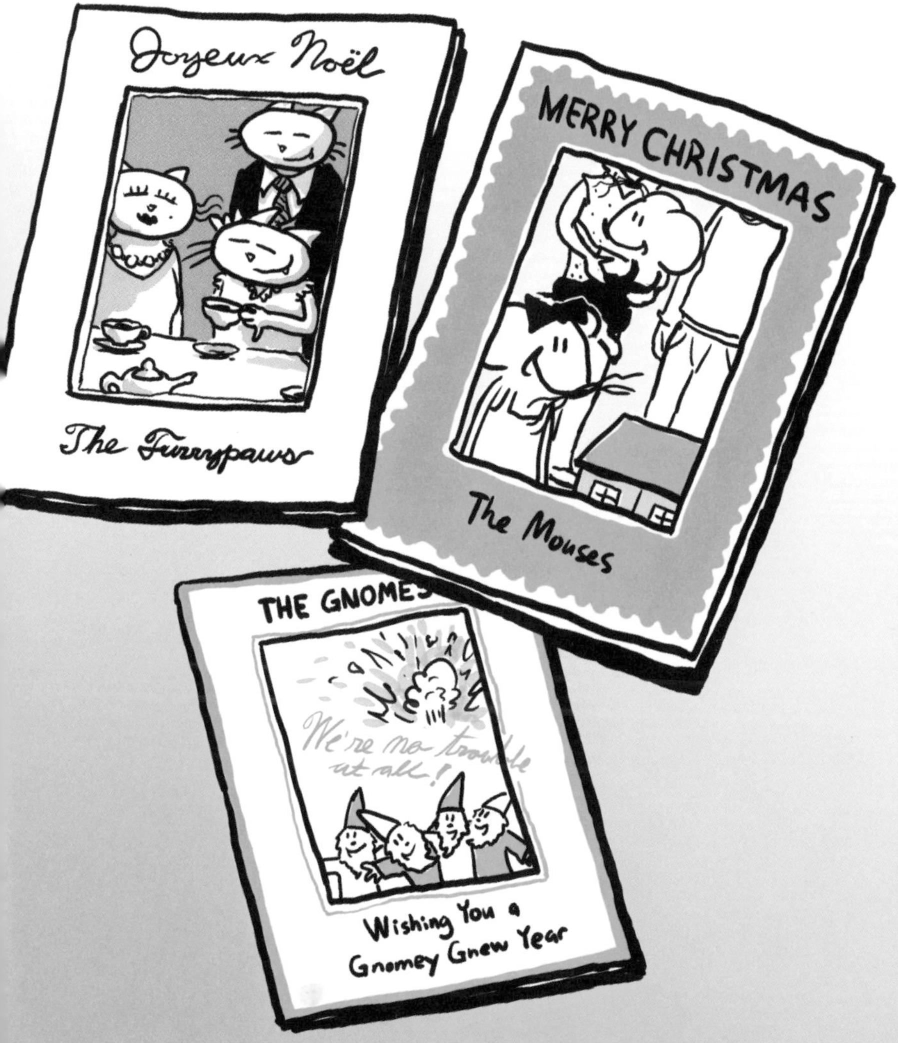

Joyeux Noël
The Fuzzypaws
MERRY CHRISTMAS
The Mouses
THE GNOMES
We're no trouble at all!
Wishing You a Gnomey Gnew Year

DON'T MISS THE NEXT BABYMOUSE!

BABYMOUSE FOR PRESIDENT

COMING IN AUGUST 2012

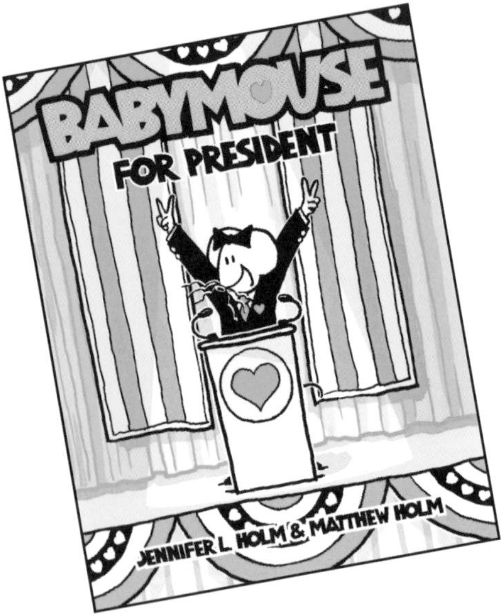
BABYMOUSE
FOR PRESIDENT
JENNIFER L. HOLM & MATTHEW HOLM

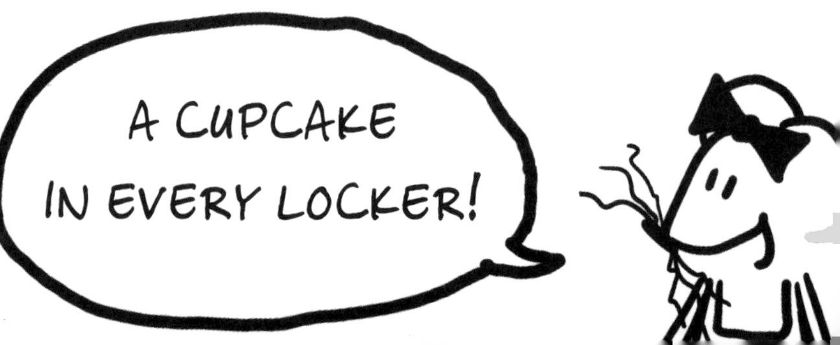
A CUPCAKE IN EVERY LOCKER!

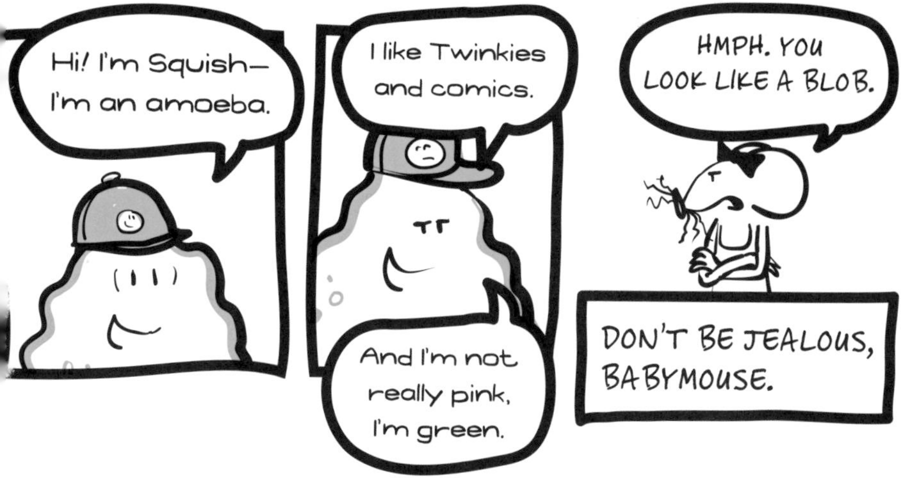
Hi! I'm Squish—
I'm an amoeba.
I like Twinkies and comics.
And I'm not really pink, I'm green.
HMPH. YOU LOOK LIKE A BLOB.
DON'T BE JEALOUS, BABYMOUSE.

READ ABOUT SQUISH'S AMAZING ADVENTURES IN:

#1 SQUISH: Super Amoeba

#2 SQUISH: Brave New Pond

AND COMING IN MAY 2012:

#3 SQUISH: The Power of the Parasite

★ "IF EVER A NEW SERIES DESERVED TO GO VIRAL, THIS ONE DOES."

– **KIRKUS REVIEWS**, STARRED

If you like Babymouse,
you'll love these other great books
by Jennifer L. Holm!

BOSTON JANE: AN ADVENTURE

BOSTON JANE: WILDERNESS DAYS

BOSTON JANE: THE CLAIM

MIDDLE SCHOOL IS WORSE THAN MEATLOAF

OUR ONLY MAY AMELIA

PENNY FROM HEAVEN

TURTLE IN PARADISE

THEY'RE
REALLY GOOD!
TRUST ME!